The Butler's Vessel

S. Rodman

Dark Angst Publishing

This book contains,

Alcohol use

Brief description of SA where the victim thinks he has consented, but he is too drunk. (Not between MCs)

Dubious Consent (Magic makes it a necessity)

Abduction for non-consent (MC is rescued in time)

Imprisonment

Tied up against will

Attempted ritual sacrifice

Contents

1. Chapter 1   1

2. Chapter 2   7

3. Chapter 3   11

4. Chapter 4   15

5. Chapter 5   21

6. Chapter 6   25

7. Chapter 7   31

8. Chapter 8   41

9. Chapter 9   45

10. Chapter 10   53

11. Chapter 11   57

12. Chapter 12   61

13. Chapter 13   69

14. Chapter 14   75

15.	Chapter 15	81
16.	Chapter 16	87
17.	Chapter 17	93
18.	Chapter 18	99
19.	Chapter 19	105
20.	Chapter 20	113
21.	Chapter 21	119
22.	Chapter 22	125
23.	Chapter 23	131
24.	Chapter 24	137
25.	Chapter 25	143
26.	Chapter 26	149
27.	Chapter 27	155
28.	Chapter 28	163
29.	Chapter 29	169
30.	Chapter 30	175
31.	Chapter 31	181
What to Read Next.		187
Want More?		191
Books By S. Rodman		192

Chapter One

E yes so dark I could fall into them forever. Strong, competent hands taking control of my body. A confident voice telling me I'm a good boy.

Lust and desire swirl within me. A gasp escapes from my very soul. My hips are dancing.

And then dazzling sunlight burns through my eyelids. The scrape of the curtains being drawn along the rail, worms into my brain.

I groan and blearily open one eye. The dream is clinging on to me and warring with the reality now assaulting my senses.

Jeeves is tying the curtains back. Seeing the man of my literal dreams is not helping me to untangle illusion from the cold light of day. I'm not sure what is real and what is not. It is disorientating.

There is a glass of water on my bedside table, as well as two ibuprofen tablets on a pretty saucer.

My head pounds. My mouth tastes like a sewer.

Ah yes. I drank too much last night, and my butler is assisting me. This is reality. Not my lover leaving my bed to open the curtains. More's the pity.

"Good morning, Master Barnaby," Jeeves says politely. "How are you feeling?"

Hungover with morning wood. Not that I'm going to say that of course. Especially as it was inappropriate dreams about Jeeves that contributed to the morning wood situation.

"Fine," I just about manage to mutter instead.

I fumble for the glass of water and gulp it down. He can't possibly know, I tell myself. There is no way in heaven or hell my butler can tell that I keep having dirty dreams about him. It is impossible.

I cast a nervous glance at him and then hurriedly snatch my gaze away. Damn it, I can feel my cheeks heating with a blush. Why does one glimpse of Jeeves's eyes have me convinced that not only does he know, but he finds it deeply amusing?

I'm just paranoid. That has to be the answer. Guilty conscience and all that. Though I shouldn't feel guilty, it's not my fault. I'm hardly choosing to have sordid and inappropriate dreams about the staff. Well, one member of staff in particular.

Perhaps I should fire him? He has only been here a year, and I damn well knew the moment I laid eyes upon him that I was going to have a problem. I should have listened to myself.

I sigh and take the ibuprofen with another swig of cold water. I can't fire Jeeves. As well as being incredibly hot, he is incredibly good at his job. And my dreams are hardly his fault.

I'll just have to suffer until I get over it. There is nothing else that can be done. Crushes don't last forever, do they?

"Prince Wilhelm of Bavaria arrived while you were sleeping," says Jeeves calmly.

Uncle Will? That's great news. I don't know him terribly well, but I enjoy his company and he seems to enjoy mine. Having a guest for the summer is going to be lovely. Something to stave off the never-ending boredom and loneliness.

"What about his guest?" I ask.

"Due to arrive soon. His Highness is anxiously awaiting."

I grin in delight. My uncle inviting an unwed vessel to stay with him for the summer is exactly the type of salacious gossip I need to spice up my life. I'm excited to meet the man who has my uncle so enthralled. And of course, the more company, the better. I do like to party.

"Would Master prefer a bath or a shower?"

The timbre of Jeeves's voice dances over my skin and makes me shiver. He is calm, confident, assured, capable. I should be the one calling him master, preferably whilst on my knees before him. But nevertheless, hearing that title on his lips does things to me. Things it shouldn't. There is something deeply wrong with me.

"Ah, yes. A bath, I think. Thank you, Jeeves," I stammer pathetically.

He nods sharply and smartly, turning the gesture into a bow of acknowledgment. Then he turns on his heels and glides silently away to prepare my bath.

Even the way he moves is hot. A heavy sigh escapes me, and I collapse back down upon my pillows.

Maybe it's a vessel thing? All the old-fashioned farts claim it isn't good for a vessel not to be wed. Perhaps they're on to something? Or perhaps it is more that I am very nearly twenty-one and still a virgin, in every sense of the word. It would be understandable if my hormones were going a little crazy.

But there is not a lot I can do about that. I am a vessel. Sex will release my magic and it will be so delighted to be free it will demand it regularly. It will seek out a mage and yearn to leave this useless body that cannot wield it, in favor of one who can.

Once I pop my cherry, I will need regular sex with a mage so I don't lose my mind, or explode. It's exactly why old fogeys believe a vessel needs to be wed to a mage.

It doesn't sound too awful, truth be told. But I'm going to become Earl Rocester in a few short months, and finding a mage who will allow me to retain my title will be a challenge. Then there will be other mages who will want to become Earl in all but name.

All in all, finding a man who doesn't just want my magic and my title is going to be impossible. And isn't that just depressing?

At least Uncle Will is here to help me fend off the swarm of unsuitable suitors who are going to descend on me this summer. It's nice of him to come, but despite my family's desire that I pretend I'm not a vessel and just concentrate on being an earl, I'm not sure that is what I want. I'm just far too much of a coward to tell anyone.

Which leaves me trapped. Being a vessel and finding a husband is tricky. Being an earl and staying single for all eternity seems ghastly. I'm a rat trapped in a maze, and every turn is a dead end.

"Your bath is ready, Master."

Jeeves's soothing voice rouses me from my depressing thoughts. A nice long soak, followed by meeting my uncle's new lover, sounds like a good day. Then in the evening I can get drunk enough to forget everything.

It is a flawless plan.

Chapter Two

It's cozy in the dining room. It's warm and the lights are low. The dark oak paneling on the walls is gleaming. The table looks incredible. All starched white linen and perfect silver. The bouquet of flowers as a centerpiece is a wonderful touch. Jeeves truly is amazing. But for once, my thoughts are fixated on someone else.

My uncle's lover is gorgeous. He has shoulder length dark hair, cheekbones to die for, and dazzling eyes that are somewhere between blue and green. There is something in the way that he carries himself that just oozes sex appeal.

I'm seething with envy. Next to him, I feel clumsy, awkward, and extremely undesirable. It is most unfair. I will never be that graceful or that alluring, and it is breaking my heart.

He also seems like a genuinely lovely person, so I can't even gloat over any personality flaws. No wonder my uncle is smitten and can't take his eyes off of him. I can't fault him for that at all.

But it is making me miserable. I'm going to die alone, I just know it. With people like Jem in the world, why would anyone ever look at me? And that's before you add in the complication that my title brings. I know I am being unreasonable, but I can't control my feelings.

It's a struggle to keep a polite expression on my face. The starter has just been served and I can tell this is going to be a long dinner. I wish I could shake off this dark mood. It is lovely to have company, and I like meeting people, especially those as interesting as Jem. I've never met a tapped yet unwed vessel before. What a wonderfully free spirit.

I should be inspired by him and the options he brings to the table. A sensible person would be peppering Jem with polite questions, to try to determine if his life choices are worth following. Since he seems happy despite being disgraced.

But all I can focus on is how hopeless I feel and how lonely I am. It seems I am turning into a self-obsessed little twerp and I hate it.

At least I got the seating arrangements right. Even if I did get into a complete tizzy over it first. But it was complicated. It is my house, but Uncle Will is a prince, so giving him the head of the table would be appropriate. But he is not an English prince, although he is older than me, as well as my uncle. And he is a mage and I'm only a vessel. I'm also only a mere lord at the moment, but very nearly an earl. But then, this is a family dinner. Or is it? Uncle Will has brought his lover, so does that make it a family dinner or not?

I'd given myself a complete headache until I just gave up and asked Jeeves. He had smoothly assured me that an informal dinner is fine and therefore I can sit at the head of the table.

It is still a relief to see Uncle Will comfortable with the seating arrangement. I should have known he would be fine, he is very laid back. I gave myself an hour of stress for no reason.

Suddenly, Jem's fork drops to his plate with a clang. The noise makes me jump.

"Are you alright?" asks Will.

"I'm fine," says Jem with a bright smile. "Just a headache. In fact, if you don't mind, I think I will retire."

"Of course. Allow me to walk you to your rooms," says Will, as he flows eagerly to his feet.

I watch them leave, and try not to feel too dismayed. I don't blame them. If I had someone to go to bed with, I wouldn't be sitting here with me either.

Uncle Will's bodyguard quietly slips out of the room. He turns in the opposite direction to the one Will and Jem took. He is clearly a sensible man who knows his trade.

And just like that, I am alone with my butler.

I take a sip of wine and try very hard not to look at Jeeves. I know he is right behind me. A slight turn of my head and I could bask in the sight of his handsome face. But I am stronger than that. It is bad enough that awareness of his presence is itching along my skin. I simply do not need to add any fuel to this inappropriate fire.

I have friends, and I have alcohol. I have everything that I need. I'm wealthy and even have a title for flip's sake. Moping because I am lonely is terribly self-pitying. People would sell their soul to be in my position.

But here I am, so fixated on my loneliness that I am pining over my butler. Which, knowing my luck, he probably is aware of, and it is probably making his job damn uncomfortable. He deserves better from me.

I down my wine and place the cup firmly on the table. A good butler would silently and unobtrusively refill it. Not

Jeeves. It is his only flaw, and damn does this indication that he cares for my well-being mess with my heart even more. I know it only means that he is a nice person. Nothing else. That knowledge does nothing to stop my foolish heart from believing it secretly means something else.

"More wine please, Jeeves."

He silently refills my cup, and I can taste his disapproval. I hate it. I want him to tell me I'm a good boy. His good boy.

The wine pours down my throat so fast that I nearly gag. I need to get a grip. So what if my butler is calm, competent, confident? I should not be losing my mind over it. I'm not a teenager anymore. I'm a grown man, nearly of age. I should act like it.

If only I knew how to.

Chapter Three

A nother night, another occasion for feeling the weight of Jeeves's silent disapproval as I drink. But this time, he's being unreasonable. It's a party for heaven's sake. A Eurovision slash my twenty-first birthday party. My guests are drinking. Uncle Will and Jem are drinking. It would be weird if I wasn't.

This is socially acceptable intoxication and Jeeves needs to bloody well get over it. He should be ecstatic that I'm not sitting alone in my drawing room, working my way through the wine cellar I inherited from my father. This is an improvement. Isn't it? Why can't Jeeves see that?

Everyone else probably thinks he is standing unobtrusively in the corner, in case he is needed. But I know. I know! Somehow his disappointment in me is swirling in my stomach, weighing it down and mixing with the wine and making me feel sick.

Damn him! I will not let him ruin my party. I live for nights like this, when the unending loneliness is held at bay, at least for a little while.

Tonight, my home is filled with people. Light and laughter. My house is not empty. I am not alone.

"Forfeit!" yells Sam gleefully.

What? I guess I haven't been paying attention. I placed a bet that the singer performing wouldn't wink at the camera, and apparently she did.

"She didn't!" I try, but my drunken friends shout me down.

"Fine!" I shout, so that they all hear me. "I accept the forfeit!"

I puff my chest up proudly. I am not a coward. I can take anything they throw at me.

"Slide down the main staircase on a tray!" bellows Roger with a naughty gleam in his eye.

I swallow. Okay, that sounds dangerous, but also super fun. And Roger seems to like me. As in, *like me*, like me. He is a mundane and completely oblivious to the world of magic, mages, and vessels, so his liking me can never lead to anything. But I still don't want to lose it. I want Roger to like me. Because then at least someone does.

"Challenge accepted!" I declare proudly.

The glint of pride in Roger's eyes makes my heart flutter. I have known him since school and he is a daft idiot. I guess I'm that desperate for any sort of attention. It certainly helps that he has no idea what a vessel is, let alone that I am one and that I'm supposed to be all lovely and charming like Jem.

To Roger, I'm just his friend from school. He is new money, I am old money. That is the only difference he can see between us. It is refreshing. I can see why my parents wanted me to go to a mundane school. To my friends I am just a soon-to-be earl, and it is as simple as that.

We stream out towards the main stairs. Sam peels off with half the group in search of a large tray. As the rest of us reach the bottom of the stairs, I look up and gulp. I swear they never used to be so tall.

"You don't have to," says Roger.

"Nonsense!" I huff. "I am Barnaby Withywood-Lamont and I never forfeit a forfeit!"

Roger laughs and suddenly I really, truly want to do this. I take a deep breath and start determinedly climbing the stairs. It seems to take forever, but finally I reach the top.

From up here, Roger and the others look frightfully far away. It is fine. I used to slide down the bannister when I was a child. No harm came to me then. This can't be much different.

Sam and his little group appear, with Sam holding a large silver serving tray above his head as if it's a trophy. I wonder if Jeeves tried to hide it from him?

Sam jogs up the stairs with enviable ease. He hands me the tray with a dramatic flourish. I bow in return.

"Thank you kind sir," I mock.

He laughs and I grin. Making people happy is my catnip. I adore it and never will be able to get enough of it.

I place the tray on the floor and climb on. Sod it. What are a few broken bones? This will be a tale that lives forever. It is worth a hospital trip.

A deep breath and a jubilant cry of "Geronimo!" and the world is whizzing past. My hair is blowing back. A shriek of terror is escaping past my lips. Gosh. I never expected it would be this fast.

I reach the bottom and continue to skid down the hallway a good few paces before finally coming to rest. I throw my body to the side, to lie on the floor, free from the tray, just in case it decides to resume motion.

I crane my neck to look at my friends. Some are leaning against walls. Others are rolling around on the floor. Everyone is laughing heartily. A huge grin spreads across my face.

That was epic.

The library is swimming around me. I must be very drunk. What is happening?

"We are playing sardines," says Roger, right by my ear.

I shiver and turn around to face him. He looks very blurry. I think it's the same night I slid on the tray, but how many hours ago that was, I could not say.

Suddenly his arms are around me. He feels warm and strong. I'm being held, touched. I sag into it. Relief flows through me. Finally, finally someone has me.

He is kissing me, and it is slobbery and messy. I don't think I like it. But being held is wonderful. It is everything I have been craving. My body needs this. My very soul does.

Roger is pulling my trousers down. I feel too hot. Too dizzy. My body is responding. But my mind is confused. I swear there is a very important reason why I should not do this. What is it? My thoughts are too slippery to catch, and Roger is warm and here and he wants me.

Someone wants me.

It's the last coherent thought I have before I spin away into the dark.

Chapter Four

Before I even open my eyes, I know everything is wrong. My magic is not a sleeping kitten, it is a panther pacing its cage. All predatory grace focused on seeking freedom.

And far less poetically, my ass is hurting.

Roger. It was Roger. He must have residual magic somewhere deep in his soul. Not enough to be sensed or used. But enough to free mine.

Oh fuck. What have I done?

"I let Roger roger me. I have been rogered by Roger. Roger gave me a good rogering," I say out loud.

The giggle that comes out of me is positively deranged. Not only have I lost my virginity, I've lost my mind.

"How are you feeling, Master Barnaby?"

I should have known Jeeves was here. I open my eyes and immediately lose myself in his dark gaze.

"Like I've been rogered," I say.

But my butler doesn't seem to get my joke. He isn't smiling. He looks solemn, serious. And sad.

"Because roger is an euphemism for butt sex and Roger is called Roger," I try to explain.

Jeeves's expression does not change. I sigh in defeat. Maybe my butler doesn't have a sense of humor. Come to think of it, I don't think I have ever heard him laugh. I always assumed he was being professional. Guess I was wrong.

"How are you feeling?" he repeats.

He is ignoring my nonsense, and I suppose that is fair enough. His question rattles around my skull. How am I feeling?

My life is over. No one will marry me now. I am disgraced. I will never be invited to any functions. No one in society will ever talk to me. All that is left is a long, lonely, isolated life.

I sob as the reality starts to hit me. "My life is over."

"Barny, look at me."

My eyes fly open in shock. Did Jeeves really just call me Barny? My heart does a ridiculous cartwheel.

His dark gaze is intense. He's so close to me, it has to be inappropriate. I could lean forward and kiss him.

"I have wrapped an incantation around you. No one will be able to tell you are tapped."

What the hell? That is not possible. Such magic does not exist. I stare into my butler's obsidian eyes and I swallow. Dark magic. It has to be. Part of me is not at all surprised that Jeeves is a practitioner of the forbidden arts. The other part of me is terrified. Of the magic, not Jeeves. Never Jeeves.

"You must never speak of it for the spell to hold."

I nod automatically. I'd do anything Jeeves told me to. That goes without saying. Then his words start to sink in. Jeeves has hidden my mistake. Covered up my disgrace. No one will ever know. My butler has saved my life. At great risk to his own.

Tears fill my eyes. "Thank you," I croak.

My arms reach for him, but he steps elegantly back, out of reach. Of course. Hugging the staff is not proper. How foolish of me to forget. My arms fall, heavy and empty, back down to my side.

"I am afraid there is nothing I can do about your need to be emptied. That will need to be dealt with the traditional way."

Oh shit. I can't believe I forgot that part of being tapped. My magic has been unleashed. It has awoken. It will grow and swell within me, and the only way to set it free is by giving my body to a mage.

Oh gods. What am I going to do?

"I can discreetly assist you," says Jeeves solemnly.

My body feels too hot. My skin is too tight. I can't remember how my lungs work, and my heart is pounding in my ears.

"Oh!" I squeak uselessly.

My butler is offering to fuck me so I don't explode. My every inappropriate fantasy about Jeeves is going to come to life. It's wonderful. It's awful. It's overwhelming.

"Thank you!" I stammer.

I don't know where to look. Or what to do with my hands. I think I'm blushing so hard I might actually burst into flames, and that would actually solve a lot of problems. Ceasing to exist would fix everything.

A few agonizing moments pass where I discover that unfortunately it's impossible to die from overwrought emotion.

"Your bath has been drawn, Master Barnaby, and when you are finished, the breakfast room will be prepared."

Right. Yes, of course. One must continue on. Stiff upper lip and all that. I have guests. I can't mope around in bed all day.

"Does Uncle Will know?" I whisper in horror.

"Yes," replies Jeeves. "He and Master James understand the need for silence."

Jem knows too? Oh my god, this is awful. Though surely if anyone were to understand, it would be him? After all, he is a disgraced vessel.

"What about my party guests?"

They won't have a clue about the magic stuff, but they might know that I slept with Roger. And if they talk, the secret will get out. No matter how strong my butler's magic is.

"They are oblivious. They each woke up this morning with a burning desire to return home. Most have already left."

Relief surges through me. I needn't have worried. Jeeves has it all under control. I wish I had handed him the reins of my life a long time ago, then I wouldn't even be in this mess.

He has done such a fine job of cleaning up after me. Disguising my mistake with dark magic. Swearing Uncle Will and Jem to secrecy. Getting rid of the other guests. There's just one problem remaining.

"Roger?" I ask weakly.

Something flashes deep in Jeeves's eyes. Something far darker than I have ever seen before. It's primal. Feral. Powerful. It raises the hairs on the back of my neck. It causes a tidal wave of visceral reaction in my body, and not all of it is fear. There is definitely something fundamentally wrong with me.

I lick my lips, swallow, and nod my understanding to Jeeves. I'm never mentioning Roger's name again. I've already forgotten it.

If only I could forget everything else.

Chapter Five

I'd rather be anywhere else in the whole entire world, than at breakfast with Uncle Will. I daren't meet his eyes. What would I see there? Disgust? Anger? Outrage? Or perhaps worse, pity?

No, I'll stare at my toast instead. It is far safer. Even though I can still feel the weight of Uncle Will's attention. It is nearly as strong as Jeeves's. I hate everything about this. I truly do wish the ground would open up and swallow me whole.

Is this my future now? I take a bite of my toast, but it tastes of nothing. Okay, time to take a deep breath. There is no need to get hysterical. Uncle Will and Jem know, nobody else does. Every other time I'm in company, it will be fine. No one else knows of my shame.

Except for Jeeves. Jeeves knows everything. And he will be with me always. As my butler, and in case I need him.

I swallow dryly. The toast refuses to go down.

I can't live like this, I can't. Lies, secrets and hidden shame. Always paranoid that someone will know.

Well, I was angsting over my future anyway. I wasn't sure if I wanted to be an earl or a vessel, since society makes it impossible to be both. Earls are manly men. Confident leaders. Vessels are demure and obedient. I think I may be more suited to the latter. And if I had a husband, there would be no need to hide the fact I have been tapped. There would be no need to be emptied by my butler.

All I need to do is trick some poor mage into marrying me, and fool him into thinking I am a virgin until after our wedding night. Then all my problems will be solved. It is quite simple, really.

This disaster could be a blessing in disguise. It has cured me of my dithering and set my feet firmly on the path of embracing life as a vessel. The fates have decided for me.

It's fine. It's all fine.

I pick up my tea and gulp it down.

Sunlight is streaming in through the large windows. It is going to be a lovely day. Hot and sunny. The best of summer. Entirely contradictory to my mood. If my emotions controlled the weather, it would be dark and stormy. Rain lashing upon the glass and an ominous rumble of thunder in the distance.

Gods, I'm being dramatic today.

Jem hurries into the room. The smile he gives Will is dazzling. My heart clenches. I very much doubt my future husband will ever look at me that way, which means no one ever will. Getting married solves a whole host of problems, but not my loneliness ones. Earls don't marry for love, not even earls who are also vessels. The best I can hope for is someone tolerable. Tolerable and pleasant. Love is so far out of the equation, it may as well not exist at all. Love is for others, not for me.

I'm not a prince who gets to take lovers on the side. Jealousy makes my tea taste bitter, but I can't help it. I'm only human.

Jem looks at me, and I make the mistake of meeting his eyes. The compassion in them hits me like a punch to the gut.

"How are you feeling, Barny?"

Oh gosh. Jem is disgraced. Probably for a stupid mistake similar to my own, yet he doesn't have a butler with dark magic to cover up his fuck-up. Unlike me, Jem has to face the consequences of his actions. And here he is, being lovely to me. He is clearly a much better person than I will ever be. It is yet another humiliation. More proof that I am simply a disaster of a human.

Jem is still watching me. Oh damn! I haven't answered him.

"I feel fine, thank you. I don't remember much about last night. I'm sorry for the inconvenience," I somehow manage to say. I think it is a polite enough response.

"Barny, you are not an inconvenience," Jem says as he sits down next to Will.

"Thank you," I mumble.

I'm not sure if I can cope with this continued kindness. It is overwhelming and entirely undeserved.

"I was thinking that I'd like to find a husband," I blurt suddenly. "Everyone says vessels are happier with a mage."

Everyone stares at me. My attempt to change the topic of conversation has certainly worked. Behind me, I sense Jeeves stiffening. I have no idea what he is thinking, but his reaction is intense. Well, intense for him. I doubt anyone else has even noticed that he has moved.

"Are you sure that is what you want?" asks Will.

I nod. "It seems like the most sensible course of action. I'd be grateful if you could let it be known that I'm open to be courted."

"Of course," agrees Will.

Uncle Will's help is a boon. At this rate, I will be married in no time at all, and my life back on track. Or rather, on a track for the first time ever. Shouldn't it feel good? Having a plan and finally knowing what direction my life is going to take?

"How about a game of tennis after breakfast?" says Will to Jem.

Me and my problems are already dismissed. I suppose it is only fair enough. What is an utter calamity to me, is just gossip to others. Not that Uncle Will is going to gossip. It is his family name too.

I stoically eat my breakfast, and Will and Jem chat and laugh and make plans for their day. After a short while, they stand up, offer me distracted farewells, and leave together. I sit back down in a heavy slump.

Jeeves smoothly steps forward and refills my cup of tea.

"Thank you, Jeeves," I say softly.

If it wasn't for my butler, I'd be utterly alone. I'm half tempted to ask him to come sit at the table and join me, but I suspect he would politely decline. I just have to make do with his comforting presence, hovering somewhere behind me.

It is the only thing I have.

Chapter Six

The sun is still shining and my mood is still darker than the abyss. I'm trailing around after the surveyor who was booked months ago. He is telling me all the very many ways the East Wing is falling down.

Jeeves is with me. He wouldn't normally be, and I'm hoping he is here because he cares about me and is concerned about my well-being. But perhaps he just thinks I'm too frazzled to pay attention to the surveyor. Or he wants to keep an eye on the spell he has woven over me. The surveyor is a mundane, so I guess this is a safe trial run.

I cast a discreet glance behind me and see Jeeves diligently taking notes. He even has a clipboard. So that answers that then. He thinks I'm not paying attention. And he is right. I know the East Wing is important, and I have no wish for it to collapse. But I just can't concentrate.

"Are there craftsmen available who know how to replace these types of beams?" Jeeves asks the surveyor.

The middle-aged man's blue, bespectacled eyes flick to me for a moment, before turning to Jeeves and latching onto him as the one who is paying attention and has sensible questions. As he launches into an explanation of how houses have not been constructed the way Rocester

Hall was, for three hundred years, I wander away to look up at one of the grand windows.

My finances are healthy, but I'm not sure they are healthy enough for all of this. Not all at once. I will probably have to choose the most essential repairs to focus on first, which means the others will get more expensive as they fall more into ruin. So it might make more sense to empty the bank balance, and do everything at once after all.

I can feel a headache coming on. Wearily, I turn back to face Jeeves and the surveyor. They are deep in conversation. Which gives me the rare opportunity of being able to stare at my butler appreciatively. He is a damn good looking man. Tall, well built, yet slender. Perfect, obsidian dark hair. Thick and shiny and styled in some sort of choppy cut. His warm skin tone and the shape of his eyes hint at some Asian ancestry, but I don't know if that is true. I strongly suspect he is not entirely human, so it could be paranormal genes giving him his looks.

Shifter of some sort? Vampire? Siren? He never seems agitated on the full moon. I see him in full daylight all the time. I've never noticed any affinity for water or singing. So I doubt it is any of those.

Fey ancestry, perhaps? Or Demon? I shudder. Whatever his lineage is, it is none of my business, so I should stop pondering it. He is simply Jeeves, and that is all that matters.

From this angle, I can admire his defined cheekbones. If he looked at me, I'd see his night-dark eyes.

I like it when he looks at me. Even though I tend to get all flustered. I wonder what it would be like to fall into those dark depths whilst being filled by him?

Oh, my gods! What is wrong with me? Where on earth did that positively filthy thought come from?

I spin around to face the window again, just in case anyone looks over and wonders why I am suddenly the same color as a tomato.

I need to think about something else, anything else. But my stomach is fluttering with the thought that sooner rather than later, I'm going to find out what it is like to be taken by Jeeves.

Will I get to look into his eyes? No, that is far too intimate. He will be helping me, not making love. He will probably want me bent over. A shiver races through my body, leaving goose pimples in its wake. I have no idea if it is trepidation or anticipation.

I suspect it's both, because I am clearly depraved. First, I get drunk and give away my virginity. Now I'm looking forward to being emptied by my butler.

"Master Barnaby?"

Jeeves's voice makes me jump out of my skin and all but levitate three foot into the air. Oh my. I need to go over to Jeeves and get involved in a conversation about structural repairs.

My treacherous feet carry me over to my butler, without me being anywhere near mentally prepared.

"Yes?" I say with my best politely enquiring tone.

The surveyor starts talking at me about guttering and downpipes. It is a struggle to keep an interested smile on my face. He starts walking towards the door, and a floorboard sags underneath him. He stops mid-sentence, and starts stomping and jumping on the floor in various spots.

It's a breather for me. A chance to gather my wits. Even though it is terrible that there is also something wrong with the floor.

"Are you feeling well, Master?" Jeeves whispers softly to me.

I flinch. I love that he cares. I hate that he has noticed that I'm behaving more of an idiot than usual.

"I'm fine, thank you, Jeeves." I whisper back.

The surveyor scribbles frantically on his fancy tablet. The technology looks incongruous on him. He very much looks like a pencil-behind-the-ear type.

"What's the verdict?" I ask.

Mostly just to demonstrate that I am capable of paying attention and asking sensible questions.

"It's going to need a thorough investigation by a dry rot team. They will need to pull a couple of floorboards up to get a proper look."

I sigh inwardly. That all sounds rather expensive.

"How soon can that be arranged?" asks Jeeves.

He has clearly seen that I have run out of intelligent sounding things to say, and he is stepping in to save me. As he always does. I really have no idea why he puts up with me. He is an excellent butler, he could get a job anywhere, and it would not be hard to find someone who is far less work than I am.

With that miserable thought ringing in my head, I trail after my butler and the surveyor as they move towards the door and continue their conversation without me.

Hopefully, it won't take too long to walk around the rest of the East Wing, and then I will be able to flee to my rooms. And have Jeeves bring me some tea.

Now, that does sound nice. Perhaps the day won't be so awful after all.

Chapter Seven

My head is pounding with a terrible headache. The breakfast table is swimming in front of me. I can't taste my toast. I can't concentrate.

It's been three days since my indiscretion, and while I doubt I'll ever be happy about it, I don't think I'm so hysterically distraught that I am giving myself a headache.

Wriggling around to a new position on my chair doesn't seem to be helping either. Perhaps it is the breakfast room that is the problem? It is lovely and quiet in here, but it is quite bright.

Uncle Will walks in and takes a seat opposite me. Guilt floods through me. How could I have forgotten the frantic phone call I received last night? Colby, Jem's brother-in-law, called me to say that Jem had been sent by the council to be emptied by someone else.

I had told Will, and he had stormed off in a rage, presumably to go fetch Jem. And here I am, moping and feeling sorry for myself.

I look up from my toast. "How is Jem?"

"Fine," Will says with a smile. Then he peers closely at me. "How are you?" he asks.

I give him a weak smile. "I'm fine, thank you. My social calendar is filling up nicely. I was wondering if you would attend some events with me?"

"Of course!" he says brightly as he pours himself a coffee.

A faint clinking sound fills the room. Oh, my spoon is rattling against the edge of my cup as I stir my tea.

"Perhaps Master should return to his bedchamber," suggests Jeeves.

A shudder wracks my body so hard that my teeth clatter. No. It can't be. Surely it is too soon? It's only been three days.

But the droning words of my boring old trainer start to replay in my mind. "When a vessel is first tapped, their magic is erratic. It eventually settles down to a predictable rhythm, with seven days being the most common, but until then, one's new husband must stay close by. It is why honeymoons exist."

Oh, my gods. Is Jeeves correct? Am I ripe? Is this what it feels like? Is my magic brimming? Demanding freedom? Is sex with a mage the only thing that can make me feel better?

A slow, careful assessment of my body confirms all of those things. I'm ripe. I'm horny. It is true.

My butler is offering to help me.

I drop my spoon and flush a bright red. "Umm . . . er . . . Yes, that is a splendid idea. Please excuse me, Uncle Will."

I clamber to my feet, turn sharply on my heels, and shuffle away with Jeeves stalking behind me like a dark shadow.

"What do I do?" I babble, as soon as we are in the hallway and out of earshot of my uncle.

I have received very basic training on what it means to be a vessel, and the practicalities involved, but right now there is nothing in my mind but blind panic.

"May I suggest retiring to your bedchamber as a good first step?"

Ah yes. Of course. How blindingly obvious. He already told me this. I am such an idiot. I pick up the pace and flee to my bedchamber.

It is dark in here. The curtains have been drawn. Jeeves must have already been in to make preparations.

I try to swallow, but my throat is too tight. My awareness of Jeeves is like a thousand tiny pinpricks all along my skin. I'm too hot. I'm too cold. I can't possibly turn around and look at him. My lungs are faltering. Breathing is so complicated when you think about it.

"Do you wish to prepare yourself, or shall I?"

The heat of my blush spreads across my cheeks and down my neck. It is burning. At least he isn't calling me master now. There is security in formality, but there is also coldness. And I don't think I could cope with that. Not that I am coping with this.

"I . . . er . . . I can do it," I mumble, as I run into my bathroom.

I lock the door and try to remember how to breathe. It's fine. Everything is fine. I'm getting to have sex with my crush. It's great. It needs to be done and everyone says sex is fun. I'm no longer a virgin. There is no reason to fall apart. Everything is good.

No one will ever know.

No one will ever know that I let my butler rail me. Not that I imagine Jeeves rails. He is probably very calm and methodical.

Oh gods. Oh gods. Oh gods.

Deep breaths. Come on now, passing out in the bathroom would be far more humiliating than anything else that is going to happen today.

Breathe. Just breathe.

My gaze falls onto the bottle of lube on the bathroom shelf, nestled amongst the soap and shampoo. It never used to be there. Jeeves is being efficient again. And the thought of that is sending my stomach into cartwheels.

As I turn away from the sight, I come face to face with a pair of soft cream pajamas, neatly laid out on the heated towel rail. My body recoils. My heart sinks. The high quality pajamas symbolize everything that is wrong. If I was about to be emptied by my husband, I'd be wearing a traditional receiving gown.

Instead, these pajamas seem to be glaring at me accusingly. They are a stark declaration of my unwed shame. My disgrace. I may be lying and hiding it from the world, but I am still a fallen vessel. Tapped, yet unwed.

Nobody would want to have anything to do with me if they knew. I'm going to be tricking them all. But I can't trick myself. I can never forget what I am. And my butler knows the truth. He knows exactly what I am.

Jeeves has given no sign of it, but he has to be deeply disappointed and ashamed of me. Does he look at me and feel disgust?

I stagger towards the toilet. I think I'm going to be sick.

I heave dryly, but nothing comes up. My head is pounding. I'm seeing flashes of color. I need to get this magic out of me. Shame and regret are going to have to wait.

I grit my teeth and reach for the lube.

A short while later, I stride into my bedroom with false confidence. Jeeves is standing by my bed, his hands clasped behind his back. His impeccable dark suit makes me feel naked in my pajamas. I cannot meet his eyes. The fake confidence that got me out of the bathroom has burned out, leaving me standing alone and deflated in the middle of the room.

"Would Master prefer to use a brace?" Jeeves asks softly.

I nod numbly.

Jeeves steps forward and places something in my hand. I stare at it. It is a finger length of wood wrapped around and around with strips of soft dark leather. Where did he get a brace from? Did he make it? That thought makes all my insides clench and my toes curl. Cold sweat is trickling down my back.

"Perhaps Master would care to bend over the bed?"

My eyes slam shut. My fists clench. The brace digs into the palm of my right hand. But Jeeves is right, it is time to get on with this. There is no point in delaying the inevitable. I made this bed, now I have to lie in it. Or in this case, bend over it.

A strange noise comes out of my nose. It's part snort laugh, part whimper. I even sound like an idiot.

Somehow my legs move. They are heavier than lead, but they carry me to the edge of my bed. I lift the brace to my mouth and clench it between my teeth. I bend over my bed and wait. The only sound in the entire world is the thumping of my heart.

"Do you remember your training?" he asks softly.

I nod and clench the sheets. My hole is all but dripping with lube, and I've opened myself up as much as I can. I hope that is what he is asking me. If he means something else, I am at a loss.

My pajama trousers are slid down, and my ability to think goes with them. I bite down on the brace and catch my pathetic whimper. Goosebumps erupt on my skin. It is not only trepidation that is coursing through my veins. Despite my nerves, I yearn for his touch, his warmth. I want him to hold me, kiss me.

But my butler is not my lover. He is only doing this out of necessity. It is going to be cold and functional. Yet still I burn for it. I crave it. I want him. Arousal is thrumming through me. My cock is hard and weeping. I am nervous and ashamed. But oh, so very desperate.

I could blame it all on the magic, but that would be yet another lie. My magic is screaming for this, but I want it too. I want my butler. I want Jeeves. Another secret to bear. Jeeves is being wonderful and saving me from my own stupid mess. He is going far above and beyond his duty. He would likely be horrified if he knew how pervertedly pleased part of me is about all of this. The poor man deserves far better than my inappropriate lust. He is not my gigolo.

One hand touches my hip, hotter than a brand. It's burning into me. Consuming me. I want that touch everywhere, but this is all I'm going to get. I feel like a man lost in the desert, catching a single drop of moisture on his tongue. I need more, so much more.

Something hot and blunt is pushing at my hole, demanding entry. Oh, my gods. It really is happening. I'm about to be filled, and this time I am going to remember it. Probably for all eternity. For every single life I am reincarnated to, I will dream of this.

My body is opening up for him.

"That's it. Good boy. You are doing so well."

The words caress my very soul. My mind short circuits. I bite down on the brace with all my might and only just stop my moan. It would have been a moan of sheer delight.

He breaches me, and the very tip of him is inside me. It already feels so good. Oh gosh. This is going to destroy me. He sinks in a little further and my body stretches around him. A yowl escapes me, unhindered by the brace. I wince. A good vessel is a quiet vessel, even I know that. I bite down harder and tighten my grip on the sheets. I will not utter another sound. I'm going to be a good boy.

"Well done. Breathe, that's it. Bear down against me, as if you are trying to push me out."

Pain flares. The stretch has turned into a burn. The brace holds my whimper in.

"You can do this."

I can do this. I am a vessel. It is what I was born for. My very purpose is to surrender my magic and my body to a mage.

He slides in some more. Panic ignites. I wish I had checked how big he was before I agreed to this plan. I'm going to be impaled. It is too much. It is never going to fit.

He pauses and makes soothing noises. I wish he'd touch me. Flip me over and kiss me.

"You can take me, Barny."

My heart flutters. My stomach flips and every muscle in my body relaxes. He called me Barny. Jeeves used my name.

He continues to slide in, and in, but the progress is easier now. Less pain, more pleasure. Warmth is shooting down my legs, causing them to tremble and my toes to curl. My breaths are coming in short, rapid bursts.

Still he gives me more, and more. Gods, how much is there? I swear if he goes any deeper, he is going to hit my ribs. Surely he has to know he is too much of a man for a novice to take? What was he thinking in offering this?

And still he eases into me. In and in, and in some more. Never ending.

Finally, I feel the press of his groin against my ass cheeks. He is all the way in. I have done it. I have taken him all. I could weep with exuberance and joy and pride.

"Well done, Barny."

A helpless groan tries to escape around my brace, but I don't let it. I'm sweating. I've never felt so full, so stretched. So complete. This feels incredible. It is nothing like the dildos I practiced with. Jeeves is so hot and heavy inside me. He is filling me to breaking point. There is no room for anything else, in my body, mind or soul. There is only Jeeves.

My lungs are heaving now. I can't remember how to open my eyes. Dull pain is seeping from my palms and my jaw. I think I'm clenching the sheets and biting down on the brace too hard.

Jeeves moves. A gentle roll of his hips that sets me alight with euphoria. Oh my, that feels good. He does it again, and again. Rocking pleasure into me with every thrust until I feel as if I am floating on a sea of it.

The friction, the pressure, the feeling of fullness, it is all divine. In my wildest dreams, I never knew it could feel like this. I finally understand why people are obsessed with sex. I think I am going to be now. My new addiction.

Thrust, and thrust. I'm soaring now. Pleasure is flooding my mind. Every inch of my skin feels alive. It is overwhelming. I want to weep, but all I can do is take it.

I can only lie here as Jeeves drives me further, and further into bliss.

A strange heat is growing low and deep within me. It feels tight and heavy. Magic? Orgasm? Both? I do not know.

Whatever it is, it is building, and building. It is making me squirm and writhe. Jeeves is keeping his steady pace. The pressure grows, and grows. It is spreading out along my every nerve ending. Consuming every single molecule of my being.

I erupt. There is no other word for it. All my pleasure, desire, and joy, pours out of me. My magic joins it. My soul is on fire. I am incandescent. I blaze in glory for long, agonizing minutes. And then I am spent.

Now I am empty and hollow. Wheezing alone as I lie here, bent over my bed. Dizziness swirls through me. I'm shaking. The intensity I just experienced has left me shattered. I can't think, can't focus.

I know only one thing.

Jeeves has left.

Chapter Eight

M y bed feels too big, too empty. But right now I can't think of anywhere else I want to be. I'm curled up in a small pathetic ball, buried under the covers, and I don't think I'm ever going to leave.

The curtains are still drawn, and it is dark and quiet in my bedchamber. I can pretend it is the middle of the night, when in reality, I have no idea what time it is and I can't bring myself to care. I'm far too busy feeling sorry for myself.

After Jeeves left me, I staggered to the shower, and then put on clean night clothes. I've stopped crying now and I've flipped the pillow over, so the tear-soaked linen is on the other side. So that's something.

I've not been completely useless. I can function a little bit. There might be hope for me yet. Though it doesn't feel like it.

I really need to pull myself together. This is my life now. For as long as it takes to trick someone into marrying me.

I don't know why I am being such a baby about it. I agreed to this plan. It is a good plan. Wanting kisses and cuddles is beyond ridiculous. The reaction of a spoiled idiot. Jeeves has agreed to help me, not pamper to my every needy whim.

I shouldn't need pampering. It wasn't my first time, even though it very much feels as if it was. Is it because I was very drunk with Roger? Or is it because Roger is Roger and Jeeves is Jeeves? I guess I'll never know.

I only know that for the rest of my life, whenever I think about my first time, I will think of this room. Of bending over this bed. Of Jeeves standing behind me.

Soft footsteps make my ears prickle. Jeeves usually moves as silently as a cat, so he has to be purposefully alerting me to his presence. Not that I need footsteps for that. His aura burns into my awareness. It always has. And now I can sense magic that was once my own, coiling within him.

A wave of disorientating nausea washes over me. I swallow. I hope he has some spell woven over himself that hides this from everyone else, otherwise our ruse that I am still a virgin vessel is going to fool no one.

He steps closer, and every muscle in my body tenses. My stomach heaves. I cannot possibly look at him. The shame is too great. He has to know how much I enjoyed being emptied. It was blindingly obvious. I do hope he didn't hate it too much, but what if he did?

The desire to crawl further under the covers and hide from my humiliation is strong. As is the urge to fling myself into his arms. What is wrong with me? Why am I such a mess?

Is all that nonsense about vessels being overly emotional and prone to hysteria true? I always dismissed it before, but perhaps this is what happens to vessels once we are tapped. We fall apart.

The urge to jump into Jeeves's arms intensifies. So much so, that my body starts to move towards him.

Okay, just take a deep breath. Calm down. Throwing myself at him will only result in him politely, yet firmly, setting me back on the bed. Regardless of whatever his feelings may be. Even if he doesn't hate me, or by some miracle is not disgusted by me, Jeeves understands the boundaries of our relationship. I need to remember them too.

And I cannot crawl further under the covers and hide from my butler. That is ridiculous. I am not a child, and he is not the monster from under the bed.

"Will Master be taking lunch in the dining room?" he asks.

As if nothing has happened.

As if he is still nothing more than my butler.

As if my entire world has not been flipped inside out and upside down.

My thoughts are scrambled. My entire being is scattered. My heart feels as if it is breaking. I am utterly lost. I'm drifting on a dark sea with no light and no compass. I don't know what I was expecting him to say, but it was not that. Anything but that.

After all the kind words he spoke to me during the deed, can he really go back to being so cold? So distant and formal? Surely not? It seems impossible. Why would he do this to me?

Unless I dreamed everything, and my butler has never touched me.

No. That is not it. I know it happened. I can feel it in my magic. I can feel it in my ass. It was not all in my imagination. Jeeves is just pretending. Maintaining a stiff upper lip. And he wants me to do the same.

"In my rooms, please," a small voice squeaks. I think it is mine. I have no idea how I remembered how to talk. Or how I recalled that he is asking me about lunch.

"Very well," he says smoothly. "Mrs. Henbury is ready to meet with you after lunch to go through the accounts."

The housekeeper. I have a meeting with the housekeeper. Okay, I understand. Jeeves is certainly giving me the message loud and clear. I'm expected to stop wallowing and carry on as normal.

And I am supposed to pretend that nothing happened. Even when we are alone together. He doesn't want me to make this weird. He doesn't want anything to change between us. He wishes to merely be my butler. With some secret extra duties that we never discuss.

It is not unreasonable of him. He is going to extraordinary lengths to ensure my life is not ruined, at great risk to himself. All he is asking of me in return is that I don't fall apart.

I can do that. I think.

I have to at least try.

I owe it to Jeeves.

Chapter Nine

I hate balls. I hate any functions in society. I never know whether to act as a soon-to-be earl or as a vessel. So I end up behaving like a complete buffoon.

Any thoughts that things might be easier, now that I have decided to embrace being a vessel, were dashed the moment the car turned into the drive of Humberland House. As I have belatedly realized that people will be expecting me to act like an earl.

A drastic change in behavior will stand out and draw attention to myself. And never mind the squirm-inducing uncomfortableness of that, how good is Jeeves's spell? Can it withstand the scrutiny of a whole ballroom full of mages?

Uncle Will and Jeeves both look at me as I wriggle in my seat, but a footman opens the door before they have a chance to say anything.

I scramble out of the car, straighten up, and smooth my suit down. The footman leads the way, and I follow blindly. Great, just great. I still don't know how to present. I'm back to being an awkward mess.

Okay, breathe. I'm here to try to attract interest. I want mages to look at me and see potential marriage material. But the last time I attended an event, I thought being an earl was my future. I'd gotten too drunk, overcompensated, and been a brash, obnoxious git.

A complete one-eighty turn from that will look suspicious, so I need to go for something in between.

My stomach heaves. Yeah, how the hell am I going to do that? It is going to be a hell of a lot easier to say than do.

At least I have Uncle Will with me. And Jeeves is going to be lurking somewhere, because bringing one's butler to a ball is odd, but I might need him, and I'm not even going to think about that! I can't possibly think of that, or I may expire on the spot.

"Are you alright, Barny?" asks Will.

"Yes! Of course! I love balls!"

I'm quite sure my smile is far too bright and that there is a manic gleam in my eyes. But I can't stop it. And now I'm thinking about *balls,* and not formal dances, and while I do love those, it is entirely inappropriate to be thinking about genitalia right now. And now I'm blushing.

"Let's get you a drink," says Will with a slight frown.

Yes, that probably is a good idea, but so embarrassing that he has so clearly seen how flustered I am.

I pause awkwardly in the hallway while Will steps forward and is announced. "Prince Wilhelm of Bavaria," causes quite a stir.

I step forward for my turn, and nobody pays me the slightest bit of attention. All eyes are still on Will and he is swarmed by people wishing to speak to him. I grab a flute of champagne from the server waiting by the entrance, then I slink past Will's crowd and search for a quiet corner.

My eyes are desperate to search for Jeeves, but I need to resist. He might not even be in the ballroom. Surrounded by this many people, I can't sense him. He may have discreetly prowled off to the servants' quarters and will hide there unless my magic goes crazy.

I gulp down the champagne so fast that the bubbles burn my nose. Please, please, any gods that are listening, please do not let me become ripe tonight. That would be awful. I'd have to find an empty room with Jeeves . . . damn! Why is this collar so tight? I can barely breathe.

Jeeves suggested waiting until my cycle settles down before venturing out, but I dismissed that idea. I need to get married as soon as possible. Before my cover is blown. The thought of waiting nearly caused me to asphyxiate with anxiety. However, in hindsight, it seems Jeeves was likely right.

I should just listen to him. It is plain stupid of me not to. He always knows what to do. He has all the sense I was not born with. Thinking that I know better is simply absurd.

None of this sudden insight can help me now. I need to get through tonight. Then I can follow my butler's advice. But he can't help me right now. The next few hours are all down to me and me alone.

My eyes fall on a large table, set in a bay window and laden with drinks. I head towards it. The trajectory takes me right past Lucien Mallory, standing unobtrusively to the side with his hoard of chaperones.

"Good evening," I say politely.

Lucien bows his head. "Good evening, Lord Rosewarne I hope you are well?"

Oh, he is being that polite and formal. I should have known. This is Lucien Mallory, after all. The most perfect vessel that was ever born. He makes me feel so inadequate, I should run away. But there is a sadness in his green eyes that I am a sucker for.

"I'm well, thank you. How have you been?" I ask.

One of his chaperones glares at me, and I glare right back. I'm a vessel too for flip's sake and even if I were not, I'm hardly going to ravish him on the dance floor.

"Very well, thank you. I recently graduated from university, and I am looking forward to my wedding in the winter."

Oh. Have I been invited? Did I decline? I don't remember. Old Blood weddings are traditionally small and discreet. It would not be surprising if I hadn't made the list. Have the invites even been sent out yet? Gosh. What the hell do I say?

"That sounds lovely," I ramble.

There, that should do it. I'm not presuming I have been invited, nor rubbing it in that I declined. It is a nice, vague comment. Perfectly safe.

"Thank you," says Lucien.

For a moment, I'm thoroughly distracted by his perfect skin and perfect dark hair. How does he do it? And he has grown his hair out since I last saw him. It is just curling around his ears now and boy, does it suit him.

Oh gosh, I think I know why he has grown it! There was a rumor going around that Count Felford was caught with his gardener, and the salacious details included that he was pulling the gardener's hair.

Lucien's hair used to be very short, now it is just long enough to grab. He is signaling that he is willing to please his future husband. In a very carnal way.

Oh no, why am I thinking about this? I shouldn't be thinking about this. I need to be thinking about anything else.

"Is your fiancé here?" I ask, for want of anything better to say. And for gods' sake, it is not exactly a change of topic. What the hell is wrong with me?

Lucien flinches ever so slightly and his eyes flick to the far corner of the room.

"I believe so," he says, in a good imitation of nonchalance.

Sympathy and dread coil together, low in my gut. If someone as perfect and beautiful and as willing to please as Lucien Mallory gets ignored by his betrothed, what earthly hope is there for me?

No. No, I need to stop being so bloody dramatic. I don't need a husband to dote on me. It doesn't matter if he never pays me any attention at all. I just need him to marry me, and have sex with me while believing it is my first time. That's all.

And chances are, my husband will like me more than Lucien's fiancé likes him. My husband is going to get to choose me, not get engaged when he is sixteen years old to a vessel of his parents' choosing. See? It's all fine.

I really need another drink. I fumble through a farewell to Lucien, which he accepts gracefully. As I step away, my eyes flick back to his and I catch him staring forlornly across the room, for all the world like a kicked puppy. I quickly snatch my gaze away. Damn it!

I reach the drinks table and gulp a flute of champagne down in one. I pick up another, and reluctantly turn back to face the room.

Count Felford is alone. Standing by a table laden with hors d'oeuvres. I'm striding over to him before I have consciously decided to.

"Why are you ignoring your fiancé?" I ask.

He raises one eyebrow and looks down his long nose at me. "Good evening to you too, Barny."

"Stop being a dick, Drew," I bristle. He is annoyingly good looking. The epitome of tall, dark and handsome. It is most unfair.

"You used to be my favorite second cousin,' he drawls languidly.

I ignore his ridiculous comment. "People are going to notice!"

"So what?" he says. "I came here to have a good time, not to be bored to death by a pompous little prick."

"You are marrying him in a few months!" I squawk in outrage. There really is no need to be so rude.

"Exactly. Need to enjoy my last few months of freedom before I am shackled to that."

Drew turns his back to me and starts heaping hors d'oeuvres onto a small plate. The set of his shoulders is down and he does seem miserable. He can be a jerk, but I honestly don't think he is a bad person.

I huff out a sigh and deflate. "Why don't you call it off, then?"

"As if my parents, or his, would allow that," he says without turning to face me.

He is not wrong. On paper, Andrew Colville, the Count Felford, and Lucien Mallory, are the perfect match. Both from old, powerful families with seats on the council but no current link with each other.

But personality wise? It is a disaster. Prim, perfect, and proper Lucien, with party loving, outspoken, often grumpy Drew? I can see why Drew is getting cold feet. Not that I can say any of this out loud.

"He is super hot. You should stop whining." Is what I say instead.

Drew finally turns back to me. His gaze flicks over my shoulder as if he is trying not to look across the room towards Lucien.

"Looks aren't everything," he grumbles.

"Duke Sothbridge seems very happy in his arranged marriage," I try.

Drew huffs as he stuffs a tiny stuffed egg into his mouth. "That was luck and you know it."

Well, Drew is clearly set on being unhappy about his upcoming wedding. It is unlikely there is anything I can say or do to change his mind.

"At least you have a betrothed," I snipe.

He lifts an eyebrow at me. "Didn't know you were looking?"

I feel myself flush and I can't think of a damn thing to say.

"Perhaps I should call it off with Mallory and offer for you instead?"

My muscles tense and my fists clench. "Thought you didn't want to get married," I snap through grinding teeth.

He shrugs. "You're not like other vessels." He pops another egg into his mouth.

My stomach clenches as if I have been punched. I despise being teased, but his last comment is worse. He means well, it was supposed to be a compliment. But it highlights all my failings. It makes it clear how everyone sees me, and I highly doubt most people will view it as a positive. Drew is probably the only one who sees it that way, and he is my cousin and already engaged.

"Rathbone is without a vessel, since Hathbury won his in a duel."

"Rathbone is at least seventy years old, and disgraced!" I splutter in outrage.

Drew just shrugs again. "What about Hyde?"

I glare at my cousin. "He is divorced because his vessel ran off with his shifter bodyguard!"

"Well, if you are going to be fussy, you will never find anyone. You are old."

Another punch to the gut. "You are a terrible cousin."

He just rolls his eyes and continues eating. He can be such an asshole. But he is only stating facts. Engagements are usually arranged when a vessel is young, with the marriage taking place on their eighteenth birthday. Drew's ploy of buying more time, by declaring that he wishes for Lucien to finish his education first, has fooled absolutely nobody. Everybody knows that he doesn't really want him.

Just as nobody, absolutely nobody, is going to want me.

To think, that I started the summer, believing I was going to need Uncle Will's help to fend off suitors, is laughable now. Laughable, cringeworthy, and embarrassing.

I'm doomed. Completely and utterly doomed.

Chapter Ten

Thoughts of the disastrous and pointless ball are filling my head. I'm never going to be able to sleep. I wish I had never gone. Uncle Will introduced me to a few people, but nobody asked me to dance. I spent the entire evening as a wallflower whilst watching Lucien and Drew pretending not to look across the room at each other.

All in all, it was a thoroughly depressing evening.

I pull the bedcovers up to my waist and try not to fiddle with them. Where is Jeeves? He always comes in once I've got ready for bed and asks if I need anything. Is he that disappointed with me? Is he avoiding me?

I aggressively plump my pillows, but I don't lie down. I'm just sitting here in bed, with the bedside lamp on. Waiting for Jeeves. As if I'm a child that needs to be tucked up at night.

Long minutes tick by. My fingers twist and untwist in my covers. The shadows in the corners of my room seem to grow darker.

After what feels like all of eternity has passed, the bedchamber door finally opens, and I blink away tears of relief. He is here. He hasn't abandoned me. Everything is as it should be. Jeeves looks like his normal stoic self, with not a hair out of place.

"Apologies for the delay, Master. There has been a development. Mr. Cambell took his leave while we were at the ball, and His Highness has doubts it was voluntary."

What the . . .? It felt awful enough leaving Jem here, but what choice did we have? He is disgraced and not welcome anywhere. And now this? He wasn't even safe as a guest in my house.

Rage flows through me. White hot and potent. Uncle Will is a prince, so it is not surprising if he has enemies, and plots against him. Or it could be his parents, unhappy that he is spending time with a disgraced vessel. Either way, it is a violation.

"Someone broke into my house and abducted my guest? How very dare they!"

Jeeves blinks at me as if he is surprised by my outrage.

"I am looking into it, Master Barnaby," he says calmly, but I can see the fire in his dark eyes.

"Good," I nod, immediately appeased. If anyone can see justice served, it is my butler. I have every faith in him. "Anything I can do?" I add.

"I will let you know if there is."

Right, of course. His words hit me like a cold bucket of water. I'm a useless, not-quite-an-earl, shambles of a vessel, who is hiding the fact they are tapped. What possible use could I be? To anyone. For anything.

The shame of that is almost enough to quench my fury. The hot and the cold war within me and leave me feeling tepid and queasy.

"Does Master require anything?"

The familiar words are comforting, but not enough to soothe the ache in my soul. They don't quell the pain caused by his dismissal of my contribution. He is even changing the conversation. Telling me in no uncertain terms that the matter is dropped.

"No thank you, Jeeves."

My butler narrows his eyes and casts a scrutinizing glance over me. No doubt he heard the despondency in my tone.

"Very well. I shall bid you goodnight then, Master Barnaby."

"Goodnight, Jeeves."

He bows his head, and then he is gone. I sigh forlornly into the empty room. He has better things to do than pander to my mood. Finding out if Jem is okay is far more important. I know this, and I know Jeeves is right about how useless I am.

But can I really just lie here and go to sleep while Jem could be in danger? Is staying out of Jeeves and Uncle Will's way the best I have to offer? Surely not. I have to think of some way to help, despite my butler's opinion. And the more I think about it, the more my earlier rage is starting to reignite.

I fumble for my phone on the nightstand. Colby answers on the fourth ring.

"What's up with Jem?" I ask without even saying hello.

Colby sighs. "I wish I knew. I love my brother-in-law, but sometimes I really think he is not right in the head."

"Do you think he will listen to you?"

"Not a chance!"

Interesting. So Jem has arrived safely at home, and given no sign that he was forced to leave under duress. I can't ask outright, because if there is an insidious plot at play, I will be putting people in danger.

"Uncle Will is devastated," I say.

Colby gives a soft laugh. "I love that my brother-in-law and your uncle might be getting together." Then he sighs despondently. "That's if they stop being idiots."

It is a small world, but then again, society is. There are only so many noble families. And it's not as if Colby is my best friend, he is just warm and lovely to everyone. I swear he is on first-name terms with everyone in the entire world.

"Yes, I wouldn't start picking a wedding outfit yet," I say. If Jem really has left of his own accord, it is not very promising for their relationship.

"No! I'm not giving up just yet! I'm sure with some meddling, all can be saved!"

"I admire your optimism," I grin, and I really do. "You are happy in your marriage, aren't you?" I add before I can stop myself. Where on earth did that come from? There seriously has to be something wrong with me. I'm supposed to be ensuring Jem's safety, not selfishly fixating on my own problems.

"I am," he agrees, and I swear I can feel the happiness pouring down the phone. "But it was a rocky start."

I do not know what to say to that. His husband, Duke Sothbridge, was notorious and widely feared. I strongly suspect "rocky," is putting it very politely.

"I heard you were on the market!" he says cheerfully.

"Thanks," I reply dryly. I should have known I am as subtle as a bull in a china shop.

"You should let me find you a husband. I'm an excellent matchmaker. Then you wouldn't need to be nervous."

I sigh heavily. "I think I'm going to need all the help I can get."

And I don't think I have ever spoken a truer word.

Chapter Eleven

The act of rolling a cigarette is as soothing as the taste of tobacco is going to be. I kick off my shoes and lie back in my recliner armchair. It is dark and quiet in my room. Just the way I like it.

I put the cigarette to my lips and realize I have forgotten a lighter. A tiny spark of magic fixes that problem, and I inhale deeply.

What a night. Jem's disappearance is deeply concerning. I hope it is a plot against Will, or Jem's brother, Duke Sothbridge, and nothing to do with Barny. But I'm going to have to do a lot of digging to make sure.

I rub my brow and try to relax. Not that I deserve to. I've been fucking everything up lately. I failed at protecting Barny. He was assaulted and tapped right under my nose. The guilt of that is far worse than my humiliation. Barny deserves far better. He is a shining light in the darkness of the world and I can't stand for that to be dimmed, not even a little.

He is being brave and strong, but he shouldn't have to be. Not if I had done my job properly. I'm here to guard him, keep him safe. I should be doing that, not fucking him.

I draw in another big lungful of nicotine, and try to banish the memories of taking Barny from my mind. He was so warm, so soft, so very responsive. It was wonderful. It was everything I have been dreaming of. It was awful. Barny did not deserve it.

And now his incredible magic is swirling inside me. Full of its unique and special flavor. Incandescent and bright. Just like Barny is.

He is flame and I am shadow. I could consume him, but then I would extinguish the very thing I am drawn to.

Barny is not meant for the likes of me. My desire is to see him settled with someone worthy. I don't get to keep him. It is not my purpose.

Another puff of smoke and I'm still not feeling any calmer. All I can see is Barny's wide blue eyes. So innocent. So kind and caring. A shining soul.

Of course, his stunning good looks don't help at all. The layers of intricate magic, woven over him since he was a child, are nothing to my eyes. I am one of the few people who can truly see him in all his fey-ancestry glory. The bloodlines are strong in him, and seem to have granted him all the extraordinary beauty of the fey race, with none of their cruelty. It is a heady combination.

One I should be man enough to resist.

I am here for one reason, and one reason only. My mission is simple. Keep Barny away from those who will want to use him for his blood. Keep him safe. Let him live his entire life thinking he is merely an ordinary vessel.

Let the bloodline extinguish with him. Though his existence is a fluke of genetic throwback, and unlikely to happen again. His children would most probably be fine. But it is not worth the risk.

It is one part of my orders I will probably succeed in, and only because Barny has shown no interest in having offspring of his own. Hopefully, I can see him married, and make sure any children will genetically be his husband and a surrogate's. Then my work will be done. My fuck up fixed.

I just need to maintain the spell hiding the fact he has been tapped, until he is wed.

And I need to keep emptying him until he has a husband to do it for him. The alternative is unthinkable.

I suck in more smoke and hold it in my lungs until I feel as if I am bursting. But I cannot deny the truth any longer. I desire him. I want Barny. I crave him. I yearn to hold him, to kiss him, for him to cling onto me and gasp my name.

I want the soft things too. Things I have never known and never will. Waking up together. Picnics. Slow dances. Lives intertwined.

Foolish dreams. I need to let them go. Let them drift away like this cigarette smoke. Those things are not for the likes of me. I am a shadow. I watch and observe. I change what needs to be changed, protect what needs to be protected. My life is not my own.

I'd be no good for Barny anyway. He needs someone like him. Someone who walks in the sunlight and not the shadows.

Another inhale of smoke. The temptation to encourage Barny to remain unwed is strong. We could continue to live here in the gentle rhythm that is our life. I could remain his butler. I could continue to empty him.

It would be one way to have him. The closest I will ever get. And it would be so easy. Barny trusts me. He listens to me. I could whisper my insidious suggestion to him and he would embrace it.

I'd get to keep him.

I wouldn't be breaking any rules. My duty is to stop anyone from discovering that fey blood runs strong in his veins. And to stop him procreating. There is nothing about making sure he has a happy life. Nothing at all.

Except my own dark and twisted conscience.

He expressed a wish to marry. It is what he wants. I want Barny to be happy. I want him to not be alone. Seeing him contentedly wed will be like a dagger to my heart, but it will also be satisfying. In a wistful way. It would be nice to know I have achieved some good with my long life.

Watching Barny's happiness will be the next best thing to having my own. It will probably be even better. And the thought of that twists and twines within me. It claws at everything I know about the universe. For it sounds a lot like love. It sounds as if I love Barny. Truly, deeply, and selfishly.

But my kind cannot love. We are not made that way.

So, what is this thing that I am feeling?

And how do I make it stop?

Chapter Twelve

M y head is spinning. My stomach hurts. I feel entirely too hot as well as too cold. I'm not too sure where I am. My thoughts are scattered like leaves on the wind.

"Master, may I suggest that you bend over the bed?"

Jeeves's calm voice cuts through the fog in my mind. My eyes fly open and find his dark gaze regarding me intently. I squirm. Reality coalesces around me. I'm standing half dressed in my bedchamber. My shirt is on but my trousers are in my hands. It's morning and I should be starting my day.

"No, I'm not ripe, I'm just unwell," I plead.

Jeeves does not release me from his stare. I whimper. My cock is hard. My body is remembering the feel of my butler's hands upon my hips, the slide of his huge cock inside me. I can't get addicted to him. This is just a temporary solution until I find a husband.

A terrible, wonderful, shameful, and delightful solution.

"I'm fine," I insist, even though my magic is raging through me.

Jeeves arches one perfect eyebrow. "I'm afraid I must insist, Master."

I whimper pathetically again, and I feel my cheeks heat. I'm not ready to do this again. Last time was too intense. It is too fresh in my mind, body, and soul. All my defenses are still weakened. He will cause me to fall apart completely.

"There is no need to be ashamed, Master," says Jeeves, with kindness in his eyes, as well as a dark desire that turns my knees weak.

I don't think he is hating his new and unexpected duties.

Oh my. If this is true, it is the most wonderful news in the entire universe. I don't want him to hate me. I want him to desire me. Even if his need is but a candle compared to the bonfire in my soul that burns for him.

Mutely, I discard the trousers I am holding and walk over to the bed. Taking a deep breath, I bend over it. I could tell myself that there is no choice, that this is the path I have chosen. But I know the truth. I know a deep, dark, and feral hunger resides within me, and my butler is the only one who can sate it.

I don't hear Jeeves move, but I swear that man is part cat. I never hear him. I only know that he is behind me because he is pulling my underwear down to my knees.

Oh, my gods. This is really happening. Again.

I shove my fist in my mouth, in a vain attempt to stay quiet. It's pointless. My butler is going to stuff me with his cock and I'm going to moan and scream. I'm going to be completely undone by ecstasy and pleasure while his soothing voice tells me how well I am doing, until I'm a sobbing, broken mess.

I can't wait.

Something drops onto the bed by my fist. I open one eye. It's my brace. Of course. I don't need to use my hand to muffle my screams, I have a brace. My butler really does think of everything.

My fumbling hand grabs the brace, and I shove it into my mouth and clench it between my teeth. The feel of it is comforting. Having something to bite down on feels like an anchor. It is something to hold on to. An illusion of security.

My train of thought scatters. My thoughts are hazy, looping things. Spinning just out of my comprehension. Dancing around me like confetti.

Somehow I catch one. It flows around me. It is realization that I am not physically prepared. Last time, I did it myself. I dimly remember recoiling at the thought of Jeeves doing it. Now I don't care. I think I'm too far gone to even find the coordination to do it myself. And I just want Jeeves inside me as soon as possible, and if this is quicker and easier, then I am all for it.

The feel of his bare hand against my naked ass cheek makes me groan. His touch is so hot it nearly burns. I swear he blazes hotter than any human should.

His fingers trace to my crack and then down to my hole. I whimper silently into my brace. His touch whispers around my rim. I can feel viscous oil. Smearing around and around my entrance. How can something so functional feel so darn good? If this prelude is unraveling what is left of my mind, the main event is going to utterly destroy me. There will be none of me left and I shall never recover.

His finger eases inside me so gently and slowly that it takes me a few heartbeats to realize it is happening. The slight pressure is a mockery of what I crave. A mere echo of what I want. I need all of him. I need him to stretch me to my limit and fill me until I feel as if I cannot breathe. I want him to possess my body, take all of me until he is the only thing that is left.

I catch my gasp with the brace as a second finger joins the first. It is still nowhere near enough, but it is better. My hips rock into it. I am supposed to stay still, as well as silent, but I can't do it. My body is no longer obeying me. It prefers my butler's commands.

But maybe it is okay? He is not my husband, he is not my mage nor my master. In fact, he calls me master. Does that mean the normal rules do not apply? Am I allowed to move? To spit out this brace and cry out his name?

No. Whatever Jeeves is, he is not my lover. I know this. I need to remember it. He is a mage and I am a vessel. Submitting to him is the natural order of things. The way it should be. I do need to stay silent and still for him. It is my duty. Surrendering my body and my magic to him is sacrosanct.

Outside of the bedroom, I am the master. Inside the bedroom, he is.

And I'm fine with that. More than fine. The horrifying secret that smolders deep within me, the one I will take to my grave, is that I long for him to be master of all of me, all of the time. Not just for emptying me.

What kind of earl desires that? Jeeves is my butler, for heaven's sake. He is staff, I am nobility. My bloodline and heritage is to rule. Not to submit. Well, only to my husband. For we are each born to our stations in life. At least, that is what I have been taught. Who am I to think that I know better than my elders? I don't think I'm so arrogant as that, yet I've long had niggling doubts about the concept of inherited rank.

A scornful laugh nearly chokes out of me. Who am I kidding? I don't hold lofty ideals. I'm just scrambling for excuses to say that it is okay that I want to be railed by my butler.

It has to be my vessel nature, getting confused by his mage status. Please let it be that. I don't want to be a twisted pervert.

Please let it be my confusing situation causing problems again. There is such a dichotomy between being an earl and being a vessel. I surely have every reason to be overwhelmed and lost. Please let me be worthy of forgiveness.

A fresh wave of pleasure washes over me, pulling my awareness back into my body and away from my tumbling and twisting thoughts.

I am here, bent over my bed. Sweating and whimpering into my brace, while my butler's fingers fill me with joy. My underwear is around my ankles and my shirt is sticking to me. My cock is hard and weeping, trapped between my abdomen and the sheets. And every fiber of my being is alight with euphoria.

His fingers leave, and my whimper pours out of me, seemingly unhindered by the brace still clenched tightly between my teeth. Need is raging through me, overtaking all my senses. I am disintegrating into nothing more than a carnal beast.

"You are doing so well," he says.

His cock nudges against my hole, and I arch my back and lift my hips up for him. I'm behaving like a wanton little whore, and most of me does not care. Because, despite everything, despite all the reasons it shouldn't, being with Jeeves just feels right. My heart and body are adamant about that. It is only my mind that is rebelling. And right now, it needs to shut the hell up. This is happening, so I might as well enjoy it.

Gentle pressure pushes against my tight ring of muscle. My body pretends to put up a feeble resistance, before giving way and letting him in. A deep, primal groan rumbles up from my lungs, and I nearly snap the brace in two to hold it back. My jaw hurts. My teeth are sinking into the leather and wood, but I did it. I didn't make a sound.

"Good boy," he whispers.

His cock slides in, and in. Filling me deeper, and deeper. Stretching me wider than I think I can take. But I am taking him. Somehow he fits inside me. My body bends to his will.

He goes deeper and deeper, but I am expecting it this time. I know how it feels to be filled by Jeeves.

I breathe, shallow and fast, as he sinks into me. Finally, I feel his groin pressed flush against my ass cheeks and another moan tries to break free from me. This one gurgles in my throat but does not make it past my brace.

His fingers curl around my hips, taking a hold of me as if he has every right to, as if I am his property, as if I belong to him.

"Well done," he says.

Then his hips move, and I writhe. He is as silent as I am, but he needs no brace. He drives in and out of me, dragging his hot and heavy cock over all the right places. I squirm, my fingers scramble for purchase in the sheets. I am keening now. The sound strange and high, caught in my throat behind the brace, but audible nonetheless. I'm too lost in pleasure to feel the shame of that.

Desire and lust flow in my veins. Every inch of me is trembling with joy. I am inhaling euphoria and exhaling bliss. Surely I have died and this is heaven? Mere mortal existence cannot feel so good.

I feel a tightening low in my guts. I can recognize it now. My peak is near. As soon as that thought crosses my addled mind, my orgasm hits me. It swells, erupts and cascades. I'm sent tumbling and crashing through an overwhelming barrage of sensations and ecstasy. I'm calling out my elation, the brace has fallen from my mouth.

My magic surges. It pours from me to Jeeves. Leaving me for one who can actually wield it. The rush leaves me dizzy. Sight and sound dim. My heart pounds. Slowly, my senses come back online.

I'm bent over my bed, almost sprawled over it. My lungs are heaving. My sweat dripping and cooling. I'm empty and hollow. My magic has gone, as has my butler's cock.

I don't need to lift my head to know that I am alone. My underwear has been pulled back up. My ass is covered. Jeeves is attempting to give me my dignity back. He left so I could compose myself.

But it feels an awful lot like being used and then abandoned. He took what he needed and then had no further use of me. The thought is unfair of me, I know it is. Jeeves is helping me.

If only my aching heart would listen to logic.

Weakly, I climb up onto my bed. My body curls up into a small ball, and I let my tears fall.

Chapter Thirteen

S unlight is streaming through the windows of my study. I'd love to be outside, in the fresh air and free. Instead of stuck in here listening to the head gardener talking about the lake's crumbling retaining wall. I'm not really following, except to note that it sounds frightfully expensive to repair. Which is the only part I really need to understand anyway.

Jeeves glides silently in, and my heart does a strange little flip. I'm always happy to see him, not that we are ever apart for long. This time my joy is increased by the thought that he might be here to rescue me. But it is also tempered by unbidden memories of the feel of his cock inside me.

I cough, and pray that it is enough to excuse my sudden blush.

"Apologies for the interruption. Baron Wyesdale is here to see you, Master Barnaby."

My gaze snaps to the calendar that is open on my computer screen. Empty space looks back at me. I'm not crazy. I don't have anything booked after this meeting with the head gardener.

Oh. My. Gosh. This can mean only one thing. Baron Wyesdale is here to court me. Traditionally. Turning up with no prior notice, as if it is still the old days, and telephones and internet haven't been invented. Though, I don't know why letters are also considered inappropriate for formal courtship. Perhaps it's so vessels are caught off guard, entirely unprepared, and completely flustered. Because that is certainly the effect.

I stare helplessly at Jeeves. My mouth opens and closes a few times, like a fish.

"I have seated Baron Wyesdale in the drawing room. Shall I bring tea?"

"Oh yes! That would be perfect!" I exclaim far too brightly.

Jeeves has saved the day once again. I'd be so lost without him.

I jump to my feet, mumble and babble my way through an apology to the gardener, and head off to the drawing room. Running my hands through my hair and straightening my clothes is going to have to do. It is rude to keep guests waiting. Even when they turn up unexpectedly.

Oh gods! I cannot recall a thing about Baron Wyesdale. Is he old? Young? Who is he related to? Is baron his subsidiary title? And when his father passes is he going to be a duke or an earl? Or is baron as high as he is ever going to rank? Does he have money? That's an important consideration, since my house is turning into a money pit.

Breathe, Barny, breathe.

I plaster a smile on my face and fling open the door to the drawing room. Baron Wyesdale politely gets to his feet, and I don't think I've ever met him before. He is not as tall as Jeeves, but he is broader. He looks late thirties to early forties. I have no earthly idea how old Jeeves is, he has one of those timeless faces.

I walk up to the baron and shake his hand. His grip is a little firm, but that is not unusual with mages. They like to assert their dominance.

"Please, have a seat," I smile.

Wyesdale smiles back, but it doesn't quite reach his blue eyes.

I'm startled to see Becky, one of the housemaids, standing quietly by the door. I hadn't noticed her when I walked in. Why is she here?

Then it dawns on me. Jeeves placed her here as a chaperone. I am officially a courting vessel, and this is officially a courtship meeting.

Uncle Will and Jem have gone to stay at Jem's home, which leaves me with only staff as chaperones. It is not ideal, but there is not a lot I can do about it. I'm more alarmed by the realization that I need to be accompanied now. It's a big change.

I swallow dryly, this all seems so irreversible. The path of being an earl and ignoring I'm a vessel, has been well and truly cut off. My decision has been enacted and I will live with the consequences for the rest of my life. Even if I change my mind right now, no one will ever see me the same way as they did before.

Jeeves walks in with impeccable timing. Tea and finger sandwiches are spread out on a silver tray he is carrying elegantly. He efficiently lays everything out on the small table between me and the baron. Then he bows his head and moves silently to the corner behind me. I'm so glad he is here.

My hands go through the motions of pouring tea, while my mind whirls. So far, Jeeves has given no indication of his opinion of Baron Wyesdale. I'm going to have to ask him later.

"It is a lovely day," I say cheerfully.

"Indeed," agrees the baron affably while sipping his tea.

"Did you have far to travel?" I inquire.

"No, just from Shropshire, and it was a pleasant journey. Your gardens are quite lovely."

The art of small talk is a well-worn groove in my mind. I let habit and routine take over, while the rest of me tries to assess the baron.

He seems nice enough so far, but of course he is going to be on his very best behavior. True character will take more than one meeting to fully figure out.

Appearance wise, he is not too old. And not bad looking either. Nowhere near as stunning as Jeeves, but very few men are.

The baron has a thick head of hair, just long enough to show a gentle wave. The deep auburn color is interesting. He is not unattractive, but could I bear to be bedded by him?

I hastily bring my teacup to my face in an effort to hide my heating cheeks. I can't believe I'm being so filthy minded. Especially when it should be the very least of my concerns.

Is he going to treat me well? Is he wealthy? Is his rank the best I can do? These are the things I should be considering. Not carnal matters. Those are irrelevant. He is a mage, he can empty my magic. That is all I need to know.

And who am I to be picky, anyway? It is frankly a miracle anyone has come calling on me at all. I should be flattered. Not assessing his body as if he were a gigolo I might choose for my entertainment.

I take another sip of tea and try to fight the truth. If I'm lucky enough to get more suitors, I'm going to compare every single one to Jeeves, just as I am doing now. And every single man is going to be found lacking. It's a reality I have to face. It is not as if I can marry my butler.

Therefore, my future husband is destined to be a failure in my heart. I need to accept that and brace myself for it.

It doesn't mean that I cannot find someone tolerable. Someone that I will be happy enough with. All hope is not lost. And I'm not losing Jeeves. He will still be my butler after I am wed. I'll still have his companionship. Just not his cock.

I nearly choke on my tea, but I manage to recover without causing a scene. There really is something deeply wrong with me. Who thinks such thoughts?

"I'd be delighted if you'd join me on Saturday. Since I've seen your lovely gardens, I'd love to show you mine," says the baron.

My cheeks heat again, this time at his ridiculous flirting. He hasn't seen any part of me at all, so I have no idea what he is talking about. At least it appears that my butler's spell is working well. If Wyesdale had any suspicion at all that I was not a virgin, he would not be inviting me.

Wyesdale stares at me, patiently waiting for an answer. My neck twitches with my longing to turn to look at Jeeves and seek his opinion. But somehow I manage to resist.

"I'd be delighted to," I say.

Because why the hell not? I can't form an opinion of Wyesdale in just one meeting, and what harm can a walk around some gardens do? At the very worst, it will be practice for me in the art of courting. And boy, do I need that.

I take yet another sip of tea, to try to quell the queasiness in my stomach. It's all going to be fine. I just know it is.

Chapter Fourteen

S aturday has come around far too fast. Jeeves has been strangely reticent in giving his opinion on Baron Wyesdale, which means things are entirely down to my own opinion. Which I don't trust at all. It's no secret that I'm not the brightest spanner in the box.

Look at me now, standing in front of my open closet, having not a clue what to wear. I can't even get dressed by myself.

"May I suggest that I accompany Master?" says Jeeves from right behind me.

I didn't even hear him come in. However, his voice doesn't make me jump, it floods me with comfort instead. I like that he is here, and I'd love nothing more than for Jeeves to come with me. But it is not appropriate.

"I can't bring my butler with me, Jeeves," I say sadly.

"It is very common for vessels to have bodyguards," he says smoothly.

I turn to face him. "But Wyesdale has already met you, he knows you are my butler."

Jeeves gives me the whisper of a smile. "It's very kind of Master, to think I would be remembered."

My heart flutters with hope. It's true, most people don't notice staff at all. If I turn up with a bodyguard, Wyesdale is very unlikely to realize my bodyguard and butler are the same person. He probably won't look twice at the man in the uniform.

Jeeves can come with me. I don't need to face this alone. And next time I go to a ball, we can do the same thing. I have no idea why Jeeves didn't think of this before, but it is brilliant.

"That would be wonderful!" I beam at Jeeves, complete with a goofy smile.

Something flashes deep within my butler's dark eyes. An emotion I cannot name, but it is something intense. It burns bright and then is gone so quickly, I am left wondering if I imagined it.

"Um . . . What do you think I should wear?" I ask.

Jeeves smiles and glides past me to start pulling clothes off of the rail. It seems he has a clear idea in mind. I'm so relieved. He really is the best butler.

The weather is perfect and the gardens at Wyesdale House are indeed lovely, and the baron is clearly very proud of them. If that makes him a little dull, I don't mind at all. To my mind, a dull husband is far better than a vicious one.

The house and the gardens are small compared to the grandeur of my home, Rocester Hall. I'm not sure if I mind that either. The baron would be getting a good deal out of the marriage, but I'd also be getting what I need. A mage to empty me. Before everyone discovers my shameful secret.

I swallow and quickly turn my thoughts away from that direction. There is no point in dwelling on that. I should focus instead on whether the baron meets my criteria.

Right, okay. What is first on my list? Probably wealth. I've already discerned that I am richer than him, in terms of property, at least. But is his lack of funds a reason to rule him out? A wealthy spouse would be nice, but I could manage without one. I think.

I wonder if the baron would be amenable to us living at Rocester Hall, or would the idea insult his manly pride? Or is he in fact coveting such things and that is the very reason he is courting me? He wants my money?

All these thoughts are enough to make me dizzy.

I'm so glad Jeeves is here. His presence is such a comfort, a source of strength even. I don't know how, since all he is doing is trailing silently and unobtrusively behind me and the baron. However he does it, I'm glad for it.

Wyesdale hasn't noticed Jeeves at all. Which, on one hand, is fantastic. But on the other, it does not say great things about his character. But then again, what noble notices staff? I can hardly fault the man for such a common flaw.

We round a corner and I blink at the sight before me. It shocks every other thought out of my mind.

A white marble statue of a woman pouring water out of a large jar, is embedded into a hollow in an embankment. The curved wall behind the statue is also white marble. Ornately carved with grapes and vine leaves.

Real water flows out of the statue's jar into a small semicircular pond at her feet. It is beautiful. To mundane eyes it would merely look like a fancy fountain.

"Is that a Revivalist shrine?" I ask with my best attempt at a nonchalant tone.

The baron gives me a scrutinizing look, as if he is trying to assess me. It is hard not to shiver under his attention.

"Ah yes, my grandfather was sadly part of that cult," he says.

Okay. So Wyesdale is claiming he is not a Revivalist. Was bringing me here a test to see if I was? Or is he merely adapting his response to what he thinks I want to hear? If I had expressed joy at the sight of the shrine, would he then have gushed forth with Revivalist beliefs?

"There used to be a portal to the fey realm here?" I ask, as if I'm impressed.

Wyesdale puffs out his chest. "Indeed. It is a very special site. Still strong in magic, as you can no doubt sense. My grandfather was convinced that with enough power it could be reopened."

I raise an eyebrow. "He truly believed the fey would be benevolent if they returned?"

"He believed that all mages, and vessels, are descendants of the fey, and as such, would be embraced and placed in power."

I stare at the baron. He doesn't sound as if he disagrees with his grandfather. Or am I just being paranoid?

"All stuff and nonsense, of course," Wyesdale says. "Thank heavens he passed away before he could do any harm. Now it is just a fountain."

I chew my bottom lip. That last bit did sound quite genuine. But Revivalists are good at hiding their opinions. I'm going to have to ask Jeeves what he thinks. There is no way I'm marrying a crazy person who thinks bringing the fey realm close enough for portals to work again is a good idea.

History is quite clear. The fey were cruel monsters. Nevermind the complete insanity of thinking it is possible to drag an entire realm back into alignment with ours.

Odd beliefs aside, the potent magic of this spot is real enough. It is tingling along my skin uncomfortably and I can feel it seeping into me. If I stand here much longer, I'm going to become ripe sooner rather than later.

"Can we move on?" I ask, while rubbing my arm.

"Of course!" gushes Wyesdale. "How thoughtless of me. I should have known a vessel would be sensitive."

He leads the way, and I force a smile onto my face. There is nothing wrong with what he said, but something about it has really annoyed me.

"How about taking tea in the orangery?" asks Wyesdale.

"That sounds lovely," I reply automatically.

It doesn't really matter where we go and what we do. We just need to spend time together to get to know one another. Wyesdale may well be my future husband. I should probably be giddy with excitement. So why do I feel so miserable?

I follow Wyesdale to his orangery. Perhaps a nice cup of tea will cheer me up. If not, in an hour or two, I'll be on my way home. And as soon as I'm alone in the back of the car with Jeeves, I just know I'll feel fine.

I just need to endure until then.

Chapter Fifteen

I pause in the doorway without letting myself be known. Watching Barny is always a joy. Even now, when he is merely sitting at his desk, scrunching his nose up at his computer screen. The light in the study is soft. Night has fallen, and it is a handful of standing lamps that are illuminating the room.

The warm glow picks up the golden hues in his hair and softens his already flawless skin. He truly is breathtaking, and I'm almost sad that I'm the only person who gets to see it. The image before me, is not even what Barny sees when he looks in a mirror.

It is a shame, but it is the way it has to be. I'm sure Barny would rather be safe than pretty. He is sensible like that. Even if he were not, I'd do it anyway. Barny's safety has come to be the most important thing in the universe to me.

The recent drama with Jem and Will was alarming. Mostly because it made me consider how I'd feel if something happened to Barny, and the answering rage I felt was frightening.

All is well, though. Jem is safe. Barny is oblivious. I know he has suspicions because he is far brighter than he gives himself credit for, but he is minding his own business. For which I am grateful. It seems my desire to protect him, stretches to me not even wanting him to hear alarming news.

Barny rubs his brow. He looks a little stressed. The open ledger by his side lets me know he is looking at his finances. He has been at it for hours. It is time for him to stop.

I step forward, and Barny looks up at me with one of his dazzling smiles. He likes me. He trusts me. It is enough to make my insides twist and my long-cold heart flutter. It is so much more than I could ever hope for. So much more than I will ever deserve.

Silently, I slide the cup of hot cocoa in front of him. His eyes light up at the sight of it, and suddenly I would do anything, absolutely anything, for him to look at me like that. I'd raze cities to the ground and turn back time. What he gives me is not enough. I am greedy for more.

I clench my fists and gather myself. This hold Barny has on me is stronger than any magic and far more dangerous. I have no idea how to fight it. I'm not even sure I want to.

He takes a sip of the cocoa and makes a soft noise of appreciation. This time my cock stirs along with my heart. How long until he is ripe again? The dark thought tears through me and leaves me ashamed.

His phone rings, and he frowns at the screen before answering.

"Why do I have to hear from other people that you are getting married?" says his mother's voice.

Barny has no idea of how well I can hear, so I keep my face blank. Not that he is looking at me. His blue eyes are glazed with sadness and he is focusing on his mother.

"I'm merely open to courting," he says softly.

"And currently courting Baron Wyesdale. You never tell me anything."

Barny sighs silently. "Sorry, Mama."

"I'm booked up for next June and July, so you can't have the wedding then."

"Yes, Mama."

"And you know I look terrible in pale colors, so you will need to choose a dark theme. It's already awful enough that I'll be the mother of the groom and everyone will assume I'm old."

"Yes, Mama."

"Make sure you find a good match, don't let the family name down."

"Yes, Mama."

"I need to go, I have guests."

"Yes . . ." says Barny, but then the line goes dead.

He puts the phone down on the desk and stares blankly at it. I could walk through the shadow realm, appear by his mother, dispatch her, and be back here before Barny would even notice I was gone.

As tempting as that thought is, I strongly suspect Barny would feel a misguided sense of grief at his mother's death. I'm going to have to think of more subtle ways to punish the woman. Creative and satisfying ways. However, that is going to have to wait. Right now, Barny needs me.

"I don't believe Baron Wysedale is a good match," I say.

Barny looks up at me in surprise. It has worked. His thoughts are no longer on his mother.

"Why not?" he asks sincerely.

He truly does care for my opinion. While believing I'm just a butler. He really is a shining soul.

"He is not wealthy enough. I believe Master can do better."

There is so much I cannot say. I cannot tell him that Wyesdale is a Revivalist. One I am certain knows nothing about Barny's fey blood, but a danger nonetheless. I cannot let Barny know that I only allowed the courtship to begin in the first place because I think permitting it to fizzle out naturally will draw far less attention than if I meddle.

"Money isn't everything," states Barny.

"Indeed, Master."

It is time to hold my tongue. I have already said too much. And I like that Barny is not obsessed with wealth. I have no wish to try to persuade him that it is important. Which leaves me nothing further I can say about Wyesdale.

Barny frowns a little at my easy acquiescence, but he does not press the matter. Instead, with a soft sigh, he turns his attention back to the computer screen. He reaches for the cup of cocoa absentmindedly. There are clear lines of weariness around his eyes.

"Perhaps it is time for bed?" I suggest.

His blue eyes flick straight to mine. Wide and full of horror. His cheeks flush full of color, and his hands tremble and spill the cocoa.

His reaction is a spear through my heart. A mortal wound I doubt I will ever recover from. The pain momentarily takes my breath away. It feels as if my world is falling. Crumbling to dust between my fingers.

He has looked at me aghast when I have needed to take him to bed to empty him. But that had seemed like shyness and embarrassment. Has this horror I am seeing now always been there, and I was merely blind to it before?

"Just to sleep," I clarify hastily.

Has submitting to me truly been so awful for him? I thought I had been giving his body pleasure, at least. And relieving him of his magic is surely somewhat appeasing.

I'm no fool, and I knew it lacked the tenderness and affection Barny hungers for and deserves. But I hadn't realized just how much he was hating it. I've found out far too late. The harm has been done.

Barny blushes even more, and snatches his attention away to trying to clean up the cocoa spillage. I whip a cloth out of my pocket, step forward, and take over.

He steps back to allow me room to work. He is so close that I can feel his body's warmth. Hear every one of his shaking breaths. He can move back further. Is the fact that he is choosing to stay this close to me a good sign? Perhaps all is not lost.

Images of holding Barny in my arms and kissing him, fill my treacherous mind. I'd love nothing more, but it would only confuse the poor boy and tangle this mess even further. Never mind that I doubt I would have the willpower to step away after tasting such sweetness. My desire to keep Barny burns strong enough as it is. I cannot feed fuel to that fire. It would consume me.

"Erm . . . yes . . . um, bed is a grand idea!" stammers Barny.

Silently, I nod and walk away. I'll lay out his pajamas and turn down his bedding. He will never know that these small acts of service are my love language and not merely my duties.

It is the only thing I can offer him.

Chapter Sixteen

The gardens look beautiful in the sunlight. Judging by the gentle way the trees are swaying, there is a slight breeze. So it is likely not too hot out there. Such a shame I can only admire it through this window.

With a heavy sigh, I look back at the letter in my hand. HMRC are opening an enquiry into my tax affairs. I haven't been fiddling my taxes at all, but I guess my accountant might have been. And even if nothing was intentional, I can still get into trouble for making mistakes. Trouble that comes with fines. Great, just great. And even if everything is correct and above board, the list of records and receipts they wish to see is huge. It is going to take me days to dig it all out and pull it together.

All in all, it is thoroughly depressing. It makes gaining a husband seem very alluring. If I was married, I could claim a weak and feeble vessel mind, and get my husband to deal with His Majesty's Revenues and Customs for me.

Suddenly, my phone buzzes in my pocket, and I nearly jump out of my skin. I fish it out and frown at the name flashing on the screen. I almost wish the ban on technology extended beyond the first meeting. Or that I had a reason not to give him my number.

"Baron Wyesdale! Good afternoon!" I say with a cheer I am not feeling.

"Please, call me Rob. There is no need for formality between us."

I'm sure he is trying to be nice and I'm being uncharitable by thinking he is being slimy and condescending.

"Erm . . . yes. Thank you Rob," I babble.

"I have tickets for the opera tomorrow night. I was wondering if you would care to join me?"

Oh gosh. Now my heart is hammering. What do I do? Jeeves has made it clear that he doesn't approve of Wyesdale, but I have no other suitors. I need to get married as soon as possible, for so many reasons, but mainly before everyone finds out I have been tapped. I have every faith in my butler's spell, but secrets have a way of worming their way out to the light of day. Besides, I haven't made my mind up about Wyesdale yet. Going to the opera is not going to do any harm, even if Jeeves believes the baron is unsuitable.

"I . . . um . . . thank you for the invitation. Regretfully, I must decline," I hear myself say. Apparently, I have decided to listen to my butler.

The shocked silence is palpable. I'm squirming. This has to be one of the most cringeworthy moments of my entire life.

"Am I correct in thinking you are ending our courtship?" asks the baron.

"Yes. Sorry!" I blabber.

The phone goes dead, and I'm far too relieved to be offended by his rudeness. And it is all the proof I need. Jeeves is right. Wyesdale is an asshole. Jeeves is just too polite to say that outright. He needed to comment on the baron's wealth instead.

Well, regardless of whether it is right or wrong, it is done. I've dumped Wyesdale and I'm back to square one. Needing a husband. But now I have precisely zero suitors.

Jeeves walks in with a tray of tea and biscuits. My eyes fix on the chocolate ones excitedly.

"I've ended my courtship with Baron Wyesdale," I say.

A ghost of a pleased smile teases at the corners of Jeeves's lips. "A wise decision, I'm sure, Master Barnaby."

My chest swells with pride, and a grin stretches across my face. Jeeves is happy with my decision. He approves. Earning his praise is the best feeling in the whole entire world.

A nameless emotion lights up his dark eyes. Something about it makes my heart flutter. I blink and Jeeves's expression is carefully blank. Nearly devoid of all feeling. Did I imagine it? I have no idea what it is I thought I saw, but I liked it. Seeing it felt like a rush.

Am I hallucinating that my butler has feelings for me? Is that what is going on?

Or, oh gods. Am I becoming ripe and my magic is growing horny for him?

No, I don't think that is it. My magic has definitely grown over the last couple of days, but it is sleeping peacefully. For now.

A strong emotion floods through me at that realization. I think it might be regret.

Seems I am a proper little deviant after all. I want to be ripe so that I have an excuse to bend over for my butler.

"Are you feeling well, Master Barnaby?"

My cheeks heat to a temperature hotter than the surface of the sun. Can he really read me like an open book? Just how many of my filthy thoughts has he discerned?

"I'm fine, just worried about this tax inspection stuff," I babble.

"I see," says Jeeves calmly. "Anything I can help with?"

A heavy, despondent sigh escapes me. "I don't think so, Jeeves, but it is very kind of you to offer."

If only he could. I'm sure he excels at taxes, just as he does everything else. But he is already going far above and beyond his duties in order to help me. I can ask no more of him. And I need to grow up and face my own problems. Not lie around waiting to be saved like some princess in a tower. Even though that does sound quite lovely.

I'd be Jeeves's princess any day.

Oh, my gods! What is wrong with me? I hastily snatch a chocolate biscuit from the tray Jeeves is still holding, and stuff it into my mouth before I forget myself entirely and say something utterly ridiculous. Thinking such things is bad enough, and knowing my bad luck, my brain-to-mouth filter will misfire and I'll start spewing humiliating nonsense at poor Jeeves, rather than only thinking it.

He keeps a perfectly straight face as he carefully sets the contents of the tray neatly down on my desk. I know I must look absurd and it is so kind of him not to laugh in my face. Though I'm sure he will the minute he is out of the room.

"Will that be all, Master?"

I'm caught helplessly in his dark gaze. I want to say "Kiss me," or "Push me against the wall and take me," but I don't. I don't say a thing. I'm not sure I'm even breathing.

Somehow, it feels as if my unspoken words are hanging in the air between us. Weighing down the very gravity.

I swear I'm seeing desire in his eyes too, but I guess I'm just hallucinating what I want to see.

Where did the sudden and intense tension come from, anyway? One minute we were talking about . . . What were we talking about? I can't even remember. Oh, yes. Taxes.

One minute we were talking about taxes and now the very air is charged. I've already assessed that I'm not ripe, so what the hell is happening? Why does it feel as if any moment now, Jeeves is going to step forward and wrap me in his arms? Why am I holding my breath and longing with every fiber of my being for him to do that very thing?

This is absurd. It has to stop. This moment of frozen time needs to end.

"No, that will be all, thank you Jeeves," I whisper hoarsely.

He blinks, and just like that, reality is restored. He bows his head, turns on his heels, and glides silently out of the room.

I suck in a huge lungful of air and try to remember how to move. But my body feels heavy and despondent. I feel rejected and hurt.

He was never about to kiss me. It was all a figment of my imagination. Feeling rejected over something that is not real, is ridiculous. But that's me all over.

Barnaby Withywood-Lamont, Lord Rosewarne and soon to be Earl Rocester. Vessel and all round ridiculous person.

No wonder I'm falling for my butler. He is the only person in the world who can put up with me.

But he'll get tired of me eventually. Everyone always does. Then I will be all alone. Forever.

No husband is ever going to be able to compare to my butler.

Chapter Seventeen

This shower isn't waking me up. It is hot and lovely, but it is no substitute for a good night's sleep. And all I did last night was toss and turn in a bed that felt far too empty and far too cold. My body ached to be held.

I've never been held, or shared a bed in my entire life, so how I can miss something I've never had, I have no idea. But I did, and I do. Not content with moping about my bed being empty, I'm now wishing I wasn't alone in this shower. I am wishing someone was pressed up close behind me.

A heavy sigh escapes me. Why am I trying to kid myself? I'm not wishing for some vague anybody. I'm longing for Jeeves. My infatuation with my butler is not fading. It's growing. Gaining strength every day. To the extent that I am now imagining him in the shower with me.

I bet he looks amazing naked. Oh gosh, naked and wet would melt my brain. Does he have abs? Of course he does. I'm sure of it. His body has got to be as perfect as the rest of him. My fingers itch to trace his every contour. I'd also like to do that with my tongue. Gods, I'd give anything to be able to lick him all over.

It is so unfair that I've had sex with him twice, yet I've never had the chance to feast my eyes upon him.

Though, he hasn't seen me naked either. Except my ass cheeks, which are probably frightfully pale. Are they flabby? Yikes, what an awful thought.

Twisting my head over my shoulder isn't giving me the best view, but to my immense relief, I think my ass looks okay. Seems surprisingly perky, in fact. Benefits of youth, I guess, because I certainly never work out. I'm far too lazy for that. Maybe I should start? Does Jeeves like ripped beefcakes?

That's a question I will never know the answer to, because I can't just blurt it out and ask him. Not in this reality. In some other dimension, where we are together, maybe I'd be brave enough.

He'd probably say something immensely soothing and reassuring, like he likes me just the way I am. I can imagine him standing behind me right now, whispering "You are beautiful," in my ear.

A shudder wracks my body. I look down at my cock. It's standing proud. Alright then. Why not? I close my eyes and start to fondle myself. Except I imagine that it is not my own hand but Jeeves's. He is standing close behind me, one hand possessively around my throat, angling my head up, and his other hand teasing my cock.

My groan echoes around the bathroom. In my imagination, it is Jeeves that starts to stroke me faster.

"Good boy," he whispers.

My knees go weak. The hot water running over my body turns into a caress. I want to lean back against Jeeves's chest, but he is not really there. So I lean forward instead and brace one hand against the wall, while still imagining that it is Jeeves's hand teasing my cock. Squeezing it. Running a thumb over my slit. Giving long firm strokes from root to tip. This carnal pleasure shooting through me is a gift from him. He wants to see me come undone in his arms. He is choosing to bring me to rapture because he believes I deserve it.

"Not yet," orders imaginary Jeeves.

I whimper as I obey him. I'm close, so very close. My balls are tight and all my muscles are trembling. Every inch of my body is crying out for sweet release. I want to fall into euphoria. I want Jeeves to catch me.

"You are doing so well."

My breaths come in rapid pants. It is so hard to do as I'm told, but I want to earn his praise more than anything in the world. I'll die trying if I have to.

"Come for me, Barny."

A high-pitched keen rings out. It ricochets around the tiled walls, far louder than the sound of the shower.

The orgasm pouring out of me is stronger than the ocean. It is blinding. All-consuming. For one timeless moment, I am falling through darkness, and pure joy is the only thing that exists.

After all eternity, I find myself leaning heavily on the shower wall and wheezing like a steam train. The water has washed away all evidence of my indiscretion. No one will ever know.

My butler will never know that I jacked off in the shower to thoughts of him.

With a shaking hand, I turn off the shower. My legs are so weak it's hard to step out of the cubicle, but miraculously I make it without falling on my ass. Somehow, I grab a towel and manage to wrap it around my waist. Drying off is going to have to wait. I'm so not up to that task right now.

Suddenly, the door flings open, and Jeeves is framed in the doorway. Anger radiates off of him. Oh gods, does he somehow know? Is he here to berate me and voice his horror and disgust? I can feel my soul already withering in shame.

His dark eyes flick to my wet and naked chest, and seem to take a while to find my face again.

"Stay here," he says. "There has been a disturbance at the perimeter."

The door shuts, and he is gone. I blink and stagger over to the toilet to take a seat. Several thoughts are whirling around my mind and making me dizzy.

Firstly, relief that I've not been caught in my dirty, perverted behavior.

Secondly, why is someone attacking my home? That makes no sense at all. And, has Jeeves been maintaining the wards all this time? I completely forgot to arrange for a mage to come and renew them. I could have asked Uncle Will while he was here. Why did Jeeves not remind me? He didn't need to take on yet another task on my behalf.

Despite the importance of all of that, there is another thought that is stealing all of my attention.

The words he just said to me are playing over and over again in my mind. He definitely didn't call me master. He was informal with me, and the delight of that is sending my heart into cartwheels. It is no doubt silly to read so much into so small a thing, but I cannot help it. Even though he was probably just flustered by the attack. But hope is hope and I'm holding onto anything I can get.

A blast of cold air hits my back and makes me yelp. A hand comes out of nowhere, wraps around my neck, and pulls me backwards. Back where the wall should be, except

I don't hit it. Instead, I fall and fall until I find myself somewhere else. My bathroom has vanished. Someone just pulled me through a portal. And now I'm standing in a very grand study. Large, lead-lined windows are before me, displaying beautiful gardens.

Gardens that I recognize. They are Wyesdale's. A hand is still around my neck, but I manage to squirm around and face my abductor. Sure enough, it is Wyesdale who glares back at me with not a trace of warmth in his blue eyes.

What on earth is going on? I cannot comprehend it. I'm dripping wet and wearing nothing but a towel that is about to fall off any minute, and I'm in Wyesdale's study. Nothing makes sense. Why would he do this?

"Why . . ." I stammer.

Wyesdale frowns and brings his free hand to my forehead, and consciousness slips away from me.

"Jeeves!" is the last thought I have before I am swallowed by the black.

Chapter Eighteen

Where am I? Waking up feels like swimming through treacle. Uphill.

This isn't my bed. But my brain isn't giving up any further information yet. All I know is that I am groggy and disoriented.

Suddenly, everything comes back in a rush. Wyesdale has abducted me.

I sit up and draw in a horrified gasp at the same time. Chains clank and my arms are restricted. I stare at the tight cuffs around my wrists. My eyes track the chains to the ring in the wall. I am chained to a bed.

I look down at my body. It is dressed in gray sweatpants and a white tee shirt. Someone dressed me while I was out cold. Someone manhandled my defenseless, naked body.

A wave of nausea washes over me. The violation feels terrifying. Did anything else happen? Panic is gripping at my lungs, restricting my ability to breathe.

My ass doesn't feel sore or stretched. I don't think I have been used, but what if I can't tell? I don't know how long I was out for. It could have been long enough for any echoing sensation to fade. And if I was unconscious, would that mean my body was so relaxed that there would be little trace anyway?

My heart is hammering. My palms are sweaty. Any minute now, I'm going to retch.

Breathe Barny. Breathe and think. Wyesdale is a mage, if he has done anything, it would have drained my magic.

Frantically, I reach for my magic and assess it. If anything, it feels stronger than last time I checked. Wyesdale hasn't emptied me. Unless I've been here for weeks, but I don't think that is true, because Jeeves wouldn't take weeks to rescue me. So therefore, Wyesdale has not emptied me. Yet.

I'm a vessel and he is a mage. He has abducted me and chained me to a bed in a windowless room. I may not be the brightest, but I'm not that dim.

I try to swallow, but my throat is too tight. Is Jeeves going to get here before Wyesdale decides to use me? I have every faith in Jeeves. I know with every part of me that he is going to move heaven and hell to get me back. Not because he loves me, but because that is who he is as a person. He thinks of me as someone in his care. Someone he needs to protect.

It doesn't mean he is going to get here in time. Wyesdale planned this. He probably has formidable wards surrounding his home, or wherever I am now.

I don't understand why he is doing this, but I believe he is capable of doing a good job of it. He doesn't appear to be unintelligent.

I draw in another shuddering breath. Why is Wyesdale doing this? Surely he is not so insulted at being dumped? He doesn't seem insane, regardless of what other flaws he has.

I'm not a particularly powerful vessel. Nor am I wealthy enough to ransom. I'm certainly nowhere near pretty enough to cause anyone's infatuation. I'm not pretty at all, just perfectly plain looking.

What does that leave? Has Wyesdale seen through Jeeves's spell and knows that I'm tapped? That is salacious gossip that would ruin my life, and make him popular for a month while everyone flocked to him for the juicy details of how he made his discovery. It is not information that would inspire an abduction. At least, not that I can see.

I'm so confused. What am I not seeing? I have to be missing something.

A sudden wave of despondency pulls me under. What does it matter? I'm here. Imprisoned. Subject to the mercy of Wyesdale's whims. Motives are irrelevant. Knowing what they are won't help me to escape.

All I can do is wait. And then endure whatever is done to me. All while hoping Jeeves comes soon.

I have never felt so powerless in all my life.

My body flinches before my mind registers that the door is opening. I take a deep breath and quash down my fear. I don't want him to see that in my eyes. I'm not giving him the satisfaction, not if I can help it.

Wyesdale steps into the small room. His eyes are cold and his expression utterly unreadable. He is looking at me as if I am no more interesting than a piece of furniture.

I meet his gaze, fight my fear, and wait for him to do something. Or say something. Anything. Because this dread coiling low and heavy through my guts is unbearable.

"I know what you are, and I know you are tapped," he says, tonelessly, as if we are discussing the weather.

I swallow. Okay, my secret is out, but right now I can't bring myself to care. In fact, I can't even fathom why I ever thought it was such a big deal. So what if people in society don't like me and don't invite me to anything. Staying home with Jeeves sounds like heaven. As long as Jeeves and I are both safe and well, nothing else matters. It's shameful that I couldn't see that before.

Wait a minute? Did Wyesdale just say, "I know what you are?" What the hell does that mean?

I need to keep my face blank. He cannot know that he has me at a disadvantage. He seems to think I know what he is on about. I mustn't hand him another card to play against me.

"I'm going to use you in a ritual on the dark moon. Cooperate and I'll let you go afterwards, and I'll keep your dirty little secret."

My heart hammers against my ribs. Any moment now, it is going to break free. A ritual? That does not sound pleasant at all. But he either requires my cooperation, or things will be an awful lot easier with them, which means he needs more from me than just an unwilling vessel chained to the middle of a casting circle. Which gives me an advantage. Finally, I have a card to play. Something to negotiate. A bargaining chip. I'm not quite as helpless as I thought I was.

"What kind of ritual?" I ask. I was aiming for sounding as if I don't care, but I think it came out sounding bored. Which is more or less the same thing, so . . . so far so good.

He lifts an eyebrow at my question as if it is the most ridiculous thing he has ever heard. My heart sinks. I've clearly made a blunder.

"One in front of the shrine," he answers dryly.

Oh shit! I can't stop my eyes from widening. He is a Revivalist, after all. Well, that explains the crazy. But why me? Is the ritual he wishes to attempt unpleasant, and he thinks I'm so desperate to keep my secret that I will suffer it and then not report him as a Revivalist?

I clench and unclench my fists. That actually makes perfect sense. Most vessels in my situation would do absolutely anything to keep their cover. Being disgraced is said to be the very worst thing that can befall a person. I certainly used to think so. It is only the last few hours that have opened my eyes to what true horror is, and how being shunned is not it.

"Oh . . . Okay," I stammer weakly while trying to look meek.

It's embarrassingly easy. Apparently, feebleness comes naturally to me. But at least it means I should be able to string Wyesdale along for a while and lure him into a false sense of security. Anything that buys Jeeves more time has to be good.

Wyesdale grins at me. As far as I can tell, he is completely fooled by my compliance. I guess he really does believe that vessels are weak. Which is great for me. Let his bigotry be his downfall.

Now, how much time do I have? Unless I have completely lost track, the dark moon is tomorrow. I guess Wyesdale factored in some time for torture in case he needed to beat me into submission.

Now that I have avoided that fate, all I have to do is wait. Wait and hope that I have bought enough time.

Jeeves has one day to rescue me.

Chapter Nineteen

S tepping through the shadows into Duke Sothbridge's sitting room takes less than a heartbeat. I find him sat on a settee, his vessel using his lap as a pillow while reading a book.

Sothbridge's eyes widen at my arrival. Understandable. Previously, I allowed him to believe that I needed him to lower his wards before I could make such an entrance.

His vessel scrambles to a sitting position and stares at me in alarm. I watch as he looks at his husband, sees the duke is calm, and then visibly relaxes himself. The duke consort clearly trusts his husband, and I find it endearing.

"I need to talk to you. Alone," I say to Sothbridge.

I have no issues with the vessel, but Sothbridge has made it clear that he wishes to protect his husband's peace of mind.

The duke nods his agreement. His vessel gets to his feet, plants a quick kiss on his husband's cheek and grabs his book before unobtrusively leaving the room.

A happy marriage then. Unusual for an arranged one. Unusual for them. Sothbridge is a dark soul. The epitome of a grump. His vessel is sunshine and light.

I want to know how it works. The urge to dissect it is strong. Taking it apart would uncover its secret mechanisms. However it functions, I should take it as hope for Barny and I, but instead cold envy is seeping into my veins. And anyway, now is not the time for seeking relationship advice.

"I am here to call in a favor," I say.

Sothbridge's eyes narrow. "I'm listening."

He doesn't look pleased, but I couldn't care less. I helped him with his brother, Jem. The duke owes me and he knows it.

"Barny has been taken," I say.

Sothbridge raises an eyebrow. "Get his uncle to help."

"His uncle is not a former Revivalist."

The duke's face pales, but he doesn't squirm or try to deny it, nor explode in rage over the fact that I know. My respect for him grows.

"I don't have anything to do with them anymore. They wanted to hurt Colby." His eyes flick to the door his vessel left through.

"I know," I agree quietly. "But you still know how they work and think."

He draws in a shuddering breath. Gathering himself. I have won his acquiescence.

"Why have they taken Barny?" He asks. It is a sensible question and a good place to start.

"He is a very powerful vessel," I lie smoothly.

Sothbridge does not need to know about Barny's fey blood. At least, not yet. It is information that I am only going to divulge if absolutely necessary.

Sothbridge's brow scrunches up in puzzlement. Clearly he has met Barny at some point.

"I have been shielding him with incantations," I answer to his unvoiced question. I don't mind him knowing that much.

Understanding flows across the duke's face. "And someone got close enough to see through it."

"Indeed," I say through gritted teeth. "Baron Wyesdale."

My failure irks me. I underestimated Wyesdale and was oblivious to the fact that he had seen Barny's fey blood. Rationally, I know it might not be my spell casting that is at fault. Wyesdale could have discovered Barny by some other means. Inside information. Whispers.

Or it might not be the reason he has taken Barny, but I can think of no other.

Whatever the motivation, I still failed to see the threat. I am a fool. And now Barny is in danger because of me. He is probably scared right now. Scared and alone. Wondering why I am not there yet.

My fists clench by my side, and I cannot relax them.

"And you cannot get through the wards?" Sothbridge asks.

"No, they are many and complex."

"Layered by a whole coven of mages, no doubt," he says thoughtfully.

That insight does make me feel slightly better. There is a reason for my incompetence. And I was right to seek help.

"How do we get through?" I ask.

"With a great deal of difficulty, and a lot of help."

I grind my teeth again. I don't have anyone else to ask. No more favors to call in. Barny's uncle will help, but if it needs more than the three of us, the mission is doomed.

Those that gave me my orders to protect Barny, will expect me to clean up my own mess. They won't care if he is hurt or used. Only that his fey blood is kept secret.

I am expected to retrieve Barny and eliminate Wyesdale. I have never wanted to obey orders so enthusiastically before. But if I cannot do it, if it is beyond my skills, I will have to contact my true masters. Wyesdale will be eliminated, but I will never get to see Barny again. I cannot even trust that my masters will allow him to live. They might decide he is more effort than he is worth.

Sothbridge tilts his head and gives me a long, considering look. It is unnerving, even though I know he cannot read my mind. Eventually he speaks.

"Just how powerful is Barny?"

"Why?" My tone is neutral but suspicion is coiling through me.

"Wyesdale has an old portal on his estate, and the dark moon is tomorrow. He may have taken Barny for far more than to merely steal a bit of extra magic. He may attempt to reopen the portal."

My mind flounders for a moment. I cast aside my annoyance that Wyesdale proudly showed off his shrine to my face. I need to concentrate on the important matters. Could Wyesdale use Barny to reopen the portal?

Barny's magic is fairly strong, but the fey essence of it could make it extremely potent for attempting to reopen a fey portal. My heart thuds. This could be far worse than I thought. I don't care about the fey conquering this realm. I care that such a casting would likely involve a sacrifice. Wyesdale doesn't merely wish to steal Barny's fey-flavored magic for his perverse fanatical rituals. He means to kill Barny.

I can feel my body trembling. Should I report to my masters? They will definitely intervene for this. The entire purpose of placing me by Barny's side was to prevent something like this from happening. But my masters' solution might be to kill Barny before Wyesdale can. Even if they do not resort to that, I will still never be allowed near him, ever again. I'm far too selfish to allow either of those things to happen. There has to be another way.

"Surely, if reopening a portal was as easy as all that, Revivalists would have achieved it centuries ago?"

I am surprised I sound so calm and level-headed when I am feeling far from it. I guess long years of practice have worn a groove for my tongue.

"When I left, people were working on feeding Wyesdale's shrine. The veil could be a lot thinner there than it was before."

"Why have you not reported this?" My composure has cracked, and that came out far too much like an angry reprimand.

Sothbridge frowns in displeasure at my accusation. "I have."

There is truth in his words, I can hear it. It appeases me, but it means whoever took his report is not doing their job. Or is a double agent. Either way, their actions, or lack of them, have endangered Barny, and that is unforgivable.

I take a deep breath and will myself to calmness. Rage and frustration will not help a thing. I need to save Barny. Then I can allow myself the luxury of emotions. And revenge.

"Do you truly believe that they might be close enough? That the dark moon and a powerful vessel will be sufficient to succeed?" I ask, focusing on the facts as I should.

The duke's expression turns thoughtful as he considers my question. I like that he is thinking it through and weighing up what he knows, and not just blurting out an opinion.

"Yes, I do believe it could," he says.

I let out a big breath. "Then we are going to need all the help we can get."

Sothbridge's eyes widen at my implication that Barny is an extremely powerful vessel. A flash of guilt burns within me and then quickly dies. It is the same thing, more or less. He is not particularly powerful, but his fey ancestry means he can still be used the same way. The details are not important. Sothbridge does not need to know them.

He gets to his feet. "I better make some calls then."

It occurs to me now, that even if Barny did not have fey ancestry, lying about his strength would still have been a good idea. Far more people are going to be willing to help prevent a potential fey invasion, than come to the aid of a vessel they don't know.

It is a sad thought, but a true one. People tend to care only about the ones they love. I'm exactly the same.

"Don't call the mage council," I say, and Sothbridge turns back to look at me. I continue quickly. "I believe they may be corrupted."

He gives me a wolfish grin. "Yes, that is clearly obvious." He doesn't seem too fazed at having to face the Revivalists and prevent a dangerous plot without the backup of the council.

It gives me hope that I won't need to report to my masters. It is all in hand. I won't need to use my very last resort.

I nod and let him leave the room to summon whatever help he can muster. Seems I am about to save Barny, and the world.

But I only truly care about one of those things.

Chapter Twenty

I have never felt more ridiculous in my life, and that in itself is ridiculous. I mean, I've been abducted. I'm being held prisoner, and here I am worrying about how I look in this white robe Wyesdale has made me wear. It's more or less an ankle length nightgown. Far more sheer than I would ever choose for myself. Not that I would ever choose anything like this in the first place.

I sigh, and try to smooth the robe down. As if that is going to make any difference. I just look absurd and that is that. A graceful and willowy vessel could probably rock this look. But I'm too stocky, too manly. Okay, not too manly in the grand scheme of things. Most people would call me a twink. I'm just not, you know, a twinky twink.

But at least Wyesdale hasn't given me a receiving gown. For one heart-stopping moment when he had presented me with this abhorrent creation, I had thought it was one.

Even though this gown isn't much different, the lack of a discreet slit at the back, from ass to ankle, is far more reassuring than it probably should be. I guess I am clinging on to what small comfort I can, and looking for hope in whatever dark corner I can find. Desperate times call for desperate measures, as they say.

It is the evening of the dark moon and Jeeves is still not here.

A shudder wracks my body just as Wyesdale unlocks the door and steps in. He is wearing a blood red cloak. His eyes track over my body and then gleam with delight. I think merely at the fact that I have complied and put the gown on.

At least, I truly and sincerely hope so. I know he intends to use me, but for some reason, the thought of him actually desiring me seems as if it would make everything far worse.

"Time to go," he says sharply.

He is all but vibrating with excitement. Whatever the hell this is, it means a lot to him.

I smile sweetly, keeping up my compliant façade, and follow him into the hallway. Nausea jiggles around in my stomach. My heart starts to race. Perhaps Jeeves is waiting until I'm outside? I can see how that would be an easier way to rescue me.

The hallway turns sharply, and I come face to face with five mages in blood-red cloaks matching Wyesdale's. These men's cowls are up and I can see nothing of their faces. The only things in the hoods are shadows.

I swallow and my feet falter. I had thought Wyesdale was alone in his plans for the dark moon. The addition of others makes this far more ominous. Is Jeeves going to be able to defeat six mages?

Wyesdale grabs my arm and starts marching me towards the back door. The five unknown mages fall into silent step behind us. It is as freaky as hell.

We reach the gardens. It's twilight. I can't help looking around for Jeeves, but I see nothing. Should I start fighting? Resisting? I steal a glance up at Wyesdale's gleeful face. No, he will just knock me out again. Then I will be of no use to anyone.

Jeeves will be here any minute, I just know he will. I have to stay brave.

I'm dragged through the gardens, towards the shrine. Trying to sneak peeks at the five mages is pointless. They are well and truly concealed by their cowls and cloaks. I wonder if they are people I know? People I trust? That thought is awful.

I turn my attention to the treeline at the edge of the gardens. It doesn't look too far. Close enough to be a taunt and tease. Should I make a run for it?

No, knowing my luck, the boundary wards will be set to keep people in, as well as out. Wyesdale has taken a prisoner after all. It would be the wise thing to do.

Besides, we have reached the shrine, and I am all out of options.

The marble seems to glow in the dusk light. A casting circle has been laid out before it. Made of white pebbles and flickering candles. It would look pretty if I wasn't so terrified.

Where is Jeeves? Talk about cutting it fine and leaving it to the last minute. I'm going to have serious words with him when this is all over.

"Lie down in the circle. Da Vinci position," snaps Wyesdale.

And he gives me a little shove towards the circle, as if I'm too dim to understand his simple instructions. He lets go of me and I step gingerly into the center of the pebbles and candles. I know damn well it is just a pretty pattern until the mages start chanting and feeding the circle with magic. But being in here is still unnerving as hell. I have goosebumps all over and the hair on the back of my neck is standing up.

If I'm going to make my own escape attempt, it needs to be now.

Because I finally see it. The configuration of the runes in this circle. The robe he has given me. The shrine, the dark moon. His five friends, making six mages in total. It has all eventually dawned on me. This is no mere ritual. This is a sacrifice.

I'm not a very powerful vessel, but sacrifices are a sure way to harvest potent power. Wyesdale is going to kill me.

I scan the treeline again.

"Get into position!" barks Wyesdale.

His tone makes me flinch. What should I do? Do I really trust Jeeves with my life? Because if I don't run now, that is exactly what I am doing.

My heart thumps. My chest feels hollow. My heart thumps again. It is right. I should listen to it. Trusting Jeeves is the right thing to do.

I take a deep breath. I lie down on my back on the grass. I spread my limbs out like a starfish. I'm just about to close my eyes when someone shrieks in terror.

Jeeves is striding out of a dark shadow by the shrine. His eyes are blazing with fury. He flings a ball of red magic into the solar plexus of the man who screamed. The red cloak billows as the mage falls to the ground.

Someone throws magic at Jeeves, but he deflects it easily. As if merely swatting a mosquito.

The five remaining mages step back. Jeeves steps forward. A coil of red magic appears around the throat of one of the men. The man's hands rise to it and he begins to desperately pull on the glowing rope of magic. None of his friends come to help him.

A blue wall of magic slams into Jeeves and pushes him back. He frowns in displeasure and it is the most terrifying thing I have ever seen. I almost feel sorry for Jeeves's enemies.

Noise and colors and the acrid smell of discharged magic. My senses are overwhelmed. Slowly my mind untangles what it is witnessing. Wyesdale and his cronies are under attack, not just from Jeeves.

Three mages are running towards us from the treeline. Jeeves brought reinforcements. I don't see Uncle Will amongst the backup, but I guess Jeeves had a reason for choosing his allies. All will become clear later, I'm sure of it.

I roll onto my stomach and commando crawl away from the battle. It is awful that I can't do more. Pathetic and frustrating. When I said I wanted to be Jeeves's princess, I didn't mean like this.

There might still be hope, though. If I keep my eyes peeled, I might be able to trip someone over or something. There might be a chance to contribute and not be utterly useless.

The fight rages on and I get a proper look at my rescuers. Duke Sothbridge, Earl Hathbury, and Lord Garrington.

Well, I'll be damned. If someone had asked me to write a list of everyone who might possibly come to my aid, these three would be nowhere on it.

Duke Sothbridge is Jem's brother and Colby's husband. I know something happened with Jem disappearing the night of the ball. Something that is none of my business.

But it explains Sothbridge's presence. He likely owes Jeeves a favor.

But Earl Hathbury? All I know of him is that he stole another man's vessel by challenging him to a duel.

As for Lord Garrington, he isn't even technically a lord at all anymore. He has been disowned for claiming his own brother as his vessel. But it turned out his brother wasn't actually his brother.

Memories of more gossip flood my mind and suddenly everything is even more confusing.

It was Garrington's father's vessel that Hathbury stole. And Garrington and Sothbridge fought a duel over Garrington's brother-not-brother. Why on earth are they all working together to rescue me?

Oh, of course. How stupid of me. I'm not important, I know that. They are here to fight the Revivalists. They are worried about the fey. Not me.

That makes sense.

The fighting intensifies, and a stray bolt of magic singes the grass by my head. I scramble backwards and whimper.

Suddenly, Jeeves's hand is on my shoulder. I look up into his dark eyes, then he is pulling me through the shadows. Time and space are bending around me. It is far more disorientating than stepping through a portal. My mind spins, frantic, bewildered, uncomprehending. Then it seeks safety in unconsciousness, and everything fades away.

Chapter Twenty-One

S eeing Barny back in his sitting room is a joy and profound relief like no other. He is curled up in an armchair, wrapped in several blankets, and holding a large mug of hot cocoa.

"Can I get you anything else, Master Barnaby?"

I think we both know I am really asking if he is okay. He looks up at me and smiles.

"I'm fine," he insists.

But I can see the lie in his blue eyes. Some of his bright innocence has been dimmed. He is physically unharmed, but there are still scars. Ones he will bear forever.

I can't stand it. I have failed him once again, and here he is smiling at me. As if I am worth forgiving. He is too good for this world. It doesn't deserve him. The desire to take him somewhere far, far away, and ensure nothing bad ever happens to him again, is strong. It is burning within me. Along with my impotent rage that anyone has dared to harm him.

"We left the others there," he says anxiously. "Are they going to be okay?"

His concern for people he barely knows is testament to what a shining light he is.

"All are well. The enemy has been defeated," I say.

He nods, accepting my statement without demanding to know how I have this information. His trust in me is explicit and undeserved. My soul is in turmoil.

I stare at him, and for the first time I don't know what to say. I have no wish to keep these walls of politeness between us. Yet, what else is there? I am his butler and his failure of a guardian. I am not his friend, and certainly not his lover.

He stares back at me, and I am lost. I'm not strong enough for this. He wants me. He may even think he loves me. But he is just a lonely boy latching onto the only available person. If I had done my job properly, kept a formal distance, he would not be seeing me this way.

It is a further result of my failure. And I want it. I want Barny to love me and only me. I yearn for him to be mine.

The way he is looking at me right now is too much. I'm not strong enough to resist. Any moment now, I'm going to crumble and pull him into my arms and never, ever let him go.

Suddenly, his magic surges. I feel it. Enticing, alluring. Calling to me stronger than any siren's song. I've been trying to ignore and deny it since I pulled him from Wyesdale, but I can't avoid the truth any longer. My heart sinks. Not now. This is unfair. Yet unsurprising. Fear and the potent magic of the shrine were bound to have an effect.

He shudders, drops my gaze, and tries to bring his cocoa to his lips with shaking hands.

"I think I may be ripe," he whispers as his cheeks flush.

Dread coils heavy and low in my guts. I can't do this to him now. It is far too soon after his abduction. He is too shaken, too vulnerable. It would be unforgivable.

"I have been lying to you," I say.

My heart clenches. He is going to hate me after this confession, and I deserve it. But I'd rather have his hate than his pain.

He gives me a quizzical look.

"Vessels are far more powerful than they are allowed to believe," I say.

He scrunches his brow. Is his magic addling his mind or have I just delivered information that is too shocking for him to take in?

"Vessels are capable of a great many things," I say, trying again. "Including the ability to give up their magic without intercourse."

He hurriedly drops my gaze and his cheeks heat again. I can sense his confusion. Guilt is tearing at me. I should have told him this from the very beginning. I should never have allowed him to believe that sleeping with me was his only option. My excuse, of not wanting to expose him to dangerous knowledge that could get him killed, is pathetic. I am a monster. In every sense of the word.

"You don't have to have sex with me to release your magic," I say in the simplest terms I can think of.

He squirms in his chair and wraps the blankets tighter around himself. His gaze is now fixed firmly on the floor.

"Is sleeping with me really that bad?" he mumbles.

My shocked and horrified gasp is audible. That is where his mind has gone? He believes I am making up excuses so I don't have to bed him? I have messed up, truly spectacularly, to have given him that impression.

I drop to my knees before him and place my hands over his, as he cradles his hot drink. He still won't look at me.

"Barny, that is not what I mean at all."

Silence.

"I don't want you to give yourself to me under false pretenses. I can teach you other ways to give me your magic."

Silence. It stretches, long and uncomfortable. The weight of it is pushing on my lungs and making it difficult to breathe.

"Why would everyone lie about how vessels function?" he asks.

He sounds weary. Bewildered and overwhelmed. It is breaking my heart. I have just destroyed the very foundations of his world, told him his whole life is a lie. All to relieve my own guilt.

Fuck. Reality hits like a bucket of ice water. What have I done? I'm such an idiot. Why can I do nothing right around Barny? Why does his mere presence evaporate every molecule of sense I have ever possessed? This is a nightmare.

"It's a long story involving subjugation, the desire to rule, and people's evil hearts," I say.

Since I cannot take back my words, the least I can do is answer him.

He sighs heavily, frees one of his hands from his mug and my grip, and rubs his brow.

"Jeeves," he says softly. "I'm . . . tired and scared and I just got home. I'm ripe and my head is pounding."

I clutch the remaining hand of his that I still hold.

"I . . . I don't want to deal with all of this right now."

That is very understandable. I truly have messed this up. In so very many different ways. It would be spectacular, if it was not so awful.

"Jeeves, please take me to bed and empty me."

My heart thuds. My mouth dries. My tongue has grown too big for my mouth. Somehow, I force it to move.

"As you wish, Master," I say.

Barny doesn't look at me but a ghost of a smile teases at his lips. The sight of it flies straight to my heart, truer than any arrow. It obliterates the last feeble brick of my former wall.

And just like that, I am done for. Truly done for.

Chapter Twenty-Two

I walk into my bedchamber on shaking legs. My magic is pulsing within me. Burning me with its desire to be free. Arousal is throbbing in my veins. My body is hypersensitive. I can feel the air moving over my skin, the rub of my pajamas as I walk.

My cock is swollen. Need and hunger are the only thoughts in my head. I want Jeeves to take me, fill me. Fuck me until I scream.

I'm not sure how much of my craving is my magic, and how much is merely my yearning for Jeeves. I'm not sure I care. It doesn't matter. Once he is inside me, everything will be perfect. He will give me the bliss I am seeking.

This desperate and unholy hunger coursing through me is a blessed relief. It has banished all my spiraling thoughts about my abduction and near sacrifice. It has chased away my confusion about whatever Jeeves was trying to tell me about vessels. All that remains is lust. Pure in its simplicity.

I reach the bed. I pull my pajama trousers down and then kick them off. I bend over and clutch the blankets.

Jeeves moves behind me. He is silent, but I can still sense him. It is as if his soul is aligned with mine. I will always know where he is. He is a part of me.

He runs a hand over my ass cheek and I shamelessly push back into his touch. I want more. I need more and I want him to know that I do. I don't want to pretend anymore. Life is too short, too precious. Mine was nearly ended tonight. I'm not wasting any more time.

No one will ever know that I moan for my butler. Not that it matters. Right now, I don't care if the entire world knows. Jeeves is incredible. I would be so very proud to be his.

No, I'm not letting my thoughts go down that dark path of thinking about all the things I cannot have. I'm going to think only of what I can have. Tonight, right now, I have the joy of Jeeves's hands on me. It is all that matters. This night is everything and I'm giving myself to it completely. This bright window of time is the only moment that exists in the vast, spinning universe.

His fingers reach my hole, and I whine. He circles sensitive flesh and bolts of pleasure shoot through my body. I'm already bucking and gasping. He has barely touched me and I am already soaring.

An oiled finger slips inside me, and I am undone. It is a mere echo of what I truly hunger for, but oh, does it feel so very good. My hips rock into it as needy whimpers spill from my mouth. I've forgotten my brace and I'm pleased. I want him to hear what he does to me.

Dimly, a small part of me objects in horror. It says I'm not in my right mind. Being ripe has caused me to lose all sense, and in the morning I'm going to be mortified by my behavior. But it is a quiet voice and easy to ignore.

One finger becomes two, and I cry out. My fists twist in the blankets. Soon I'm going to be sobbing and drooling onto my bed.

Abruptly, with no warning at all, the fingers are gone. I'm empty. The shock of it makes me gasp. I start to whine in protest, but the world spins and cuts my whimper short. I blink and try to get my bearings. I'm on my back. Jeeves has flipped me over and now I'm staring up at him. His eyes are blazing. My heart flutters and my stomach flips.

Suddenly, soft, insistent lips are on mine. I squeak in surprise. The lips move, hot, demanding, enticing. Pleasure erupts. I moan hungrily. Jeeves is kissing me. There are fireworks in my mind and fire in my veins. All my muscles are melting. His tongue claims my mouth, and it is more joy than I can take.

My hands are wrapped around him, holding him close. But he pulls away and breaks free. I stare up at him in outrage. His hand fumbles with the top button of his shirt. My eyes widen. Oh, hell yes!

My hands fly up and bat his out of the way. Then, with a dexterity I did not know I possessed, I glide down his shirt, undoing the buttons with a speed that would win me a gold medal if it were an Olympic sport.

My new-found efficiency is rewarded by the sight of Jeeves's naked chest. And it is even more beautiful than I ever imagined. I reverently lift my hand to trace the contours before me, but Jeeves pulls impatiently at my pajama top.

Oh, right. I take a lapel in each hand and yank with all my might. Buttons ping everywhere, but my chest is free.

Jeeves dives down and claims my mouth again, and this time, my bare chest is pressed against his. My toes curl and I nearly convulse with sheer joy. This is the most incredible moment of my entire life. Does pleasure such as this truly exist? Have I died and gone to heaven?

Our kiss deepens. It heats. The flames of it flow out to consume my entire body. My soul, my heart, my mind are all enthralled by the wonder of kissing Jeeves.

His hand starts to explore my naked body. Everywhere his touch trails, it ignites my already overheated skin. It is almost too intense.

His fingers brush against my aching cock and I break from our kiss to throw back my head and keen. He dances his fingers over me. A caress that is a torment. It is too light. It is a taunt and a tease. I lift my hips up in a silent plea for more, but still his fingers only dance up and down my length. My cock throbs. I sob.

He forms a fist and he tugs. My eyes roll back. I gurgle deep in my throat. I'm seeing stars, and I always thought that was a mere euphemism. I'm astonished to discover it is a reality.

He stops, and I understand. I need to peak with him inside me. He can't bring me to glory just yet.

I shuffle back on the bed and spread my legs wide for him. His dark eyes all but glow at the sight. He licks his lips and crawls onto the bed after me. A predator stalking his prey. My stomach swoops.

His trousers are gone. I don't remember that happening. I want to look down and drink in the sight of him, but I'm too lost in his eyes.

Then he leans down and kisses me again, and I forget all about seeing him. My world is sensation and ecstasy. Time ceases to have any meaning. Reality fades away. Jeeves is the only thing that exists. His scent. His touch. The feel of his skin pressed against my own. The warmth of his body. He is everywhere and he is everything.

His cock pushes at my entrance. My back arches. I am so ready for him that the need of it hurts. His hips move and I feel a burn and a sting. I take a deep breath and my body yields. A groan escapes as the first part of him breaches my tight ring of muscle. I swallow down oxygen as he sinks in. Impaling me. Stretching me wide and filling me to my very limit. It is intense. It is wonderful. It is everything I have been craving.

My legs are around his waist. My hands are clawing at his back. He is giving me more and more. Going deeper and deeper. Taking me thoroughly. And nothing, absolutely nothing, has ever felt better.

I feel the press of his hip bones against my ass cheeks. He is all the way in. Fully seated. We both gasp. Getting him all the way inside me was hard work for both of us. My body is sweating and shuddering. He is giving my body a chance to fully adjust to him, I know this. I appreciate this. But I'm still impatient.

I want him to rock his hips and rock my world.

My body twitches and writhes. I need him to move. A scream pours out of me before I consciously register the sensation. Jeeves snapped his hips back and then thrust back into me. I'm still shuddering from the shockwaves, but he has done it again. And again. And again.

Pleasure. Joy. Euphoria. Ecstasy. Rapture and bliss. He keeps filling me more and more. Each thrust takes me to a new level. I'm flying. I'm soaring. I'm falling. I'm scattered.

He has driven everything that is dark and bad far away and replaced it with shining elation. My mind, body, soul, and magic are in perfect alignment. I am at peace.

He thrusts into me again and my joy overflows. There is too much for me to contain. My ecstasy, my orgasm, and my magic, all flow out of me like the breaking of a dam, while my body trembles, clenches, and arches. I am screaming a song of my sheer and utter joy.

Jeeves holds me close while I ride the whirlwind of sensation and pleasure storming through me. His arms are strong and secure. I feel safe. I feel wanted.

My body sags as the tempest passes its peak. I don't fight the pull of the peaceful and soft dark. There is nothing to fear.

Jeeves has me.

Chapter Twenty-Three

B arny's bed is soft. The sheets are the finest Egyptian cotton. He deserves no less.

I however, do not deserve this.

His head is resting on my chest. One of his arms is flung over me, as is one of his legs. It is common for vessels to pass out after being emptied. Especially when the emptying is intense. I know he will wake up soon. I should leave before he does. I should not be stealing this one precious moment. I should never have kissed him. I should not have turned emptying into love making.

I'm lying here, waiting for guilt, shame, and regret to take hold. But I don't think they are going to make an appearance. My selfishness has finally won. Making love to Barny was the single brightest moment in my long life. It was everything I ever wanted.

And now as I lie here, savoring it, and relishing the joy of holding him, the only thoughts within me are happiness and a desire for more. The very many reasons why I shouldn't, all seem irrelevant now.

My decision clicks into place and sets in my soul, firmer than concrete. Fuck doing the right thing. I will not leave. Barny is mine. I am keeping him.

A feeling of immense peace, joy, and relief washes over me. It feels wonderful to have finally decided. And this feeling swirling within me, tells me, with no shadow of a doubt, that I have chosen the right path. The fates are pleased. This destiny was meant to be.

He stirs in my arms. His head tilts up. Blurry, blue eyes fix on me. Confusion crosses his perfect face. He licks his lips.

"Is this a dream?" he whispers.

A smile stretches my lips. "No, Barny. This is the first day of forever."

He blushes and drops my gaze. He moves his head back down into a more comfortable angle, but he makes no move to pull away or untangle our bodies.

"Are you saying you like me? As in, *like*, like?" he asks, still sounding a little dazed.

Regret and guilt finally find me. I wish I had not hidden my feelings from him. I hate that he feels such doubt. I shall have to spend the rest of our lives making it up to him. And I'm so thankful to have the opportunity to do so. I'm almost grateful to Wyesdale for giving me the fright I needed to finally come to my senses.

"My love, you are my entire world," I say.

"Oh!" squeaks Barny and I can feel his cheek heating the skin of my chest. "I'm quite sure I am dreaming," he says. "And it is my favorite dream so far."

"You have been dreaming of me, my love?" I tease softly.

He nods his head against my chest. "Every night, since forever."

I chuckle and tighten my arms around him. I had suspected, but the confirmation is still delightful. Even though I am a little sad that Barny doesn't believe this is real. I cannot blame the poor boy for that, since I have rather pulled a complete change of heart on him. He will need time to adjust. We both will. And there is no better time to start than right now.

"How does taking a boat out onto the lake sound?" I ask.

He pauses for a moment. "It sounds like a date?" he says hesitantly.

"Indeed," I agree. "We need to get to know one another. As lovers. People. Not butler and master."

He falls quiet again. His hand starts to trace the contours of my chest. I don't think he realizes he is doing it. The feel of his caress is like electricity. I want to freeze all motion so he never notices, and never stops.

"I don't even know your first name," he says softly.

He sounds sad and guilty, but he has no need to feel either of those things, and now he is mine, I do not want him to experience any unpleasant emotions ever again.

"I have answered to many names," I say. "But Jeeves is my favorite, for it is my name upon your lips."

He squirms but doesn't try to pull away. I'm not sure if I would let him. I've only just claimed him and my possessiveness is burning brightly.

"That's the most romantic thing I've ever heard," he mumbles. "I have to be dreaming."

I kiss the top of his head and exult in his soft golden hair tickling my nose. He will realize soon enough that all of this is real.

"What . . . what are you?" he asks falteringly. "I've always thought you weren't fully human."

My heart thuds so loudly he has to be able to hear it. Dread starts to run colder than ice in my veins. What if, after everything, Barny doesn't want me? I'm not sure if I could continue to live if he rejects me. But he deserves the truth. I owe him that much at least.

"I am jin," I say quietly, as if him not hearing me will somehow help.

"Oh," he says. "I've never met a jin."

Relief flows through me with an intensity that brings tears to my eyes. That is all Barny has to say on the matter? It warms my heart and strengthens my conviction that we are meant to be together. We were made for each other.

Barny is perfect, and I will spend a lifetime trying my best to be perfect for him in return.

The summer sun is sparkling on the surface of the lake. It is not as dazzling as Barny. He is sitting across from me in the boat and positively beaming. I think he still believes he is dreaming, but he has decided to embrace and enjoy it.

His loneliness and self-doubt are falling away. His love-starved soul is filling up. I wish this picnic hamper was not between us, so I could get to work on his touch-starved needs.

When he finally accepts this is not a dream, watching him blossom is going to be exquisite.

"Here is a good spot, Jeeves," he says.

I stop rowing and pull the oars up. He blushes and looks down at his lap.

"Sorry, I didn't mean to boss you around."

I let my smile stretch across my face, and the joy of being able to do so makes me smile even more. I probably look crazed. It makes me almost glad that Barny is staring resolutely down and twisting his hands in the hem of his shirt.

"I like it," I say. I hope he can hear the truth in my words.

He looks up at me. Surprise clear in his deep blue eyes. "Really?"

I nod.

He sighs. "I should still stop it. At the very least when we are alone. Which I hope will be most of the time."

His look turns nervous. "Are you staying as my butler? I shouldn't assume that we are just going to live here and change nothing else."

"I hope your looking for a husband will change," I tease.

"Of course!" he exclaims, as he returns my grin with a hundred thousand-wattage one of his own.

"Then everything else can stay exactly the same," I say.

Barny lets out a big huff as his shoulders visibly relax. He looks around at the lake and his ancestral home. "Wonderful."

I couldn't agree more.

I lean forward and open the picnic hamper. The heat of the sun is on my back. Water is lapping gently at the boat. There is not another soul in sight. This moment is idyllic. The future promises many more moments such as this.

Spending a lifetime here, with Barny, will be better than any heaven I have ever heard of. Peace. Comfort. Companionship and love. My love for him and his love for me. I am truly blessed. I will not take a single day for granted.

Carefully, I arrange a plate of cucumber sandwiches and his favorite small cakes. I do truly enjoy serving Barny. I guess it really has become my love language.

I hand him the plate I have prepared for him, and he accepts it with another bright smile. It is all the reward that I need.

I pour him a drink and then sit back with my own plate. It is a strange feeling, this happiness and contentment bubbling through me.

I'm very much looking forward to getting used to it.

Chapter
Twenty-Four

I am starting to think this might not be a dream.
Forty-eight glorious hours in Jeeves's company.
Including spending the entire night sleeping in his arms.

My imagination is filthy. I would not have come up with
a chaste night of snuggling. That, and the amount of detail
I am experiencing over a prolonged period of time, are
indicating that this is all real.

Jeeves is now my boyfriend.

Unless, I died and this is my personal heaven?

I look up from the book I am pretending to read. My
feet are on Jeeves's lap while he reads a newspaper. We are
sharing the settee in my sitting room. The sun is starting
to set but the sky outside of the window is still light. A fire
is crackling in the hearth, because it is cozy and I wanted
one, even though it is summer. Not that the thick stone
walls of Rocester Hall ever pay any heed to the seasons, so
a fire isn't even wildly excessive.

If I am dead, I don't care. Not even one little bit. This is
everything I need. Every single thing I have ever wanted. I
have never been happier.

I will stay here forever. Unwed. If people discover that I am tapped and that my butler is my lover, it won't bother me at all. Jeeves is my world. I don't need anyone or anything else. Living in Rocester Hall in splendid isolation, will be no hardship at all.

Jeeves puts his newspaper down and looks at me. The poor man was probably suffocating under the weight of my stare. I still can't look away. I get to look at him now. I don't have to snatch my gaze away and pretend I'm not ogling, and I'm going to take full advantage of it.

He smiles at me and my heart flutters. "What would you like for dinner?" he asks.

It's hard not to answer, "You," but I just about manage to keep it to myself. I have no wish to be quite that corny. Even though it's true. I'd love nothing more than to take Jeeves in my mouth. Hopefully, he will allow me to do it soon. Maybe even tonight.

Oh no! Now I am blushing and he probably can tell exactly what I am thinking, so I might as well have said it anyway.

"Roast chicken!" I blurt in an effort to hide my tracks.

He gives me a truly naughty smirk that tells me that he has seen right through me. He carefully removes my feet from his lap and he stands up.

"I'll go tell Rupert," he says.

"Thank you."

Maybe I should hire a new butler. Then I will get to keep Jeeves all to myself and he will never have to leave my side. It really is a most tempting idea.

Jeeves takes a step away from me, and then freezes. His back goes rigid. His fists clench by his side but it doesn't even look as if he is breathing.

"Jeeves?" I ask as I pull myself from my sprawl to a sitting position.

A purple portal opens right in my sitting room, and one short woman and three hulking men stroll through as if they have every right to. I'm spluttering in outrage and indignation even before I recognize the gray suits that signify the mage council.

"What is the meaning of this?" I demand, as I jump to my feet. "Do you have a warrant?"

The woman all but flings a piece of paper at me. I scowl at her and hurriedly cast my eye over it. It looks legitimate, but I have no earthly idea what a warrant is supposed to look like.

"Release my butler at once!" I order sharply.

The woman smirks at me. "I'm afraid that is not possible, Earl Rocester. We are here to arrest him."

My heart thuds, but I concentrate on narrowing my eyes. I bet this woman knows damn well I have not been investitured yet, and is playing some sick mind game by forcing me to admit that I'm only a lord at the moment. Well, fuck her. I'm not playing that game.

"On what charge?" I snap, as if I cannot imagine anything more ridiculous than my butler being guilty of anything.

"Practicing dark magic," she says triumphantly.

I will myself not to pale. This cannot be happening. Wyesdale and his cronies saw Jeeves wielding dark magic. But how on earth could they report it without revealing that they had abducted and were trying to sacrifice me? Unless they have given some twisted allegation that hides the truth?

"That is preposterous!" I huff.

She smiles at me. All teeth and no warmth. "Questioning will only take a few hours, my lord. Then we will have him back by your side."

I draw myself up to my, admittedly not very tall, full height. "No! I do not permit you to take him. He is my staff member, under my protection, in my home."

I wish I could see his face. He is frozen in a magic trap with his back to me. Is he scared? Is there something he needs me to do? Does he have any ideas, because blustering and protesting is all I have.

"I'm afraid the warrant supersedes all of that, my lord. I am terribly sorry. We will try our best to keep your inconvenience to a minimum."

I glare at her and her smug little face. She has me and she knows it. If I were truly convinced that my butler was innocent, I'd be annoyed that he was being taken away for a few hours, but that would be all.

"This is an insult!" I rage. "You are implying that I am too incompetent to know that my butler practices the dark arts! Of course I would know!"

Her eyes narrow. "Are you sure you wish to go down that road, my lord?" she whispers, as if we are co-conspirators.

This time I can't stop myself from paling. I probably look whiter than a ghost. Getting arrested alongside Jeeves won't help matters at all. I can't free him if I'm locked up too. And aiding and abetting the dark arts is a serious charge.

"He is innocent!" I stammer. "Wyesdale is merely enraged that I turned down his offer of marriage."

Her eyes flash with interest. So it is quite likely Wyesdale then. Clearly, whatever Jeeves's allies did to him was not enough of a deterrent. The man needs teaching a serious lesson. Unless this is Jeeves's allies betraying him. I know what self-serving snakes most people are.

"Earl Rocester, I am sure you are correct about your butler's innocence. But we must investigate such serious allegations, I'm sure you understand that. We will have him returned to you in no time at all."

With that, her two burly companions step forward. I watch helplessly as they each take one of Jeeves's frozen arms, lift him up, and carry him towards the portal.

"I'll get you out, Jeeves!" I call desperately. I don't even know if he can hear me.

My heart stops beating the moment he is taken into the portal and disappears from sight. The woman gives me another smug smirk and then she also steps into the portal. It winks out of existence behind her and suddenly I am all alone in my sitting room.

What are they going to do to Jeeves? Will he be able to hide his dark magic from them? Will they be able to tell he is jin?

I try to swallow, but my throat is too tight. Every muscle in my body is constricted with the horror flowing in my veins.

He won't be able to escape. I know that much. The council chambers are one of the most heavily warded places in the world.

So how the hell am I going to get in?

Chapter Twenty-Five

I can't stop pacing the parlor. Back and forth, back and forth. All it is going to achieve is wearing a groove in the carpet, but I cannot stay still.

I look out of the window again. Still nothing. Frustration gnaws at me. Every minute feels like a year. Time is not on my side, but I can't do a thing until Drew gets here. I'm powerless, useless. Jeeves could be under torture right now, and all I am doing is wearing my carpet out.

Finally, a flash of headlights lets me know someone is coming down the drive. I turn and run out of the parlor, down the hall. I explode out of the front door, down the steps. I'm running across the gravel, and I fling myself into Drew's arms the moment he steps out of his car. He grunts in surprise, as well as from the impact.

"Barny, what the hell is going on? You sounded hysterical on the phone."

I draw in a shuddering breath and try to gather some words. But there is so much to say. So much to explain, and it is all whirling around my head in a big tangled mess.

Drew pushes me away from his chest and holds me at arm's length. He frowns as he looks at me and the state that I'm in. Then his eyes flick to the open front door.

"You need tea. Where is your butler?"

Air rushes into me. It wheezes past my throat. It burns my lungs. I gasp and then I burst into tears.

Drews swears in alarm. I'm dimly aware of Mrs. Henbury hurrying out of the house. She barks an order at Becky. Then Drew and Mrs. Henbury work together to get me back into the parlor and seated in a comfortable chair. Becky comes in with tea and a steaming cup is placed in my hands. Reflexively, I sip at it.

The door softly closes and I am alone with Drew. My tears dry up. Numbness has taken over from hysteria. Thank heavens.

"You are scaring me, Barny. What the hell is going on? Why has your butler been arrested?"

I blink at my cousin. Mrs. Henbury must have told him that much while they were manhandling me inside.

"On charges of dark magic, but it is all part of a sinister plot and I have to save him!" I blurt.

I'm sprouting incomprehensible gibberish, but at least I can now talk. This is great. My entire plan hinges on my ability to talk.

Drew's brows scrunch in confusion. "You are quite sure your butler is innocent?"

"Oh no, he does use dark magic, but he is harmless. Well, he doesn't wish to harm anyone. I don't think."

Drew is staring at me. His eyes are wide and his face is pale. Any minute now, he is going to call for me to be locked up for insanity.

I take a deep breath and try again. "Baron Wyesdale is a Revivalist. He abducted me and was going to sacrifice me in a ritual. Jeeves used dark magic to rescue me, and I don't know if it was Wyesdale and his cronies, or if one of Jeeves's allies has turned on him, but someone reported him to the council."

Drew blinks slowly at me. "That's . . . quite something. Have you told the council this?"

"No! Because they can't be trusted!" I wail in frustration.

Drew says nothing, but I can see the weary acknowledgement in his eyes. He knows the council is a nest of vipers.

"It is lovely that your butler was loyal enough to save you, but dark magic is dark magic, Barny. Perhaps you should let the council do their thing?"

I set my tea down with shaking hands. "No!" I say resolutely. "I love him. Jeeves is my lover, and I will not leave him in the hands of the council."

The look of incredulous shock that explodes over Drew's face is almost amusing. He stares at me in shocked silence for a long, agonizing moment. Then he lets out a low whistle.

"Always the quiet ones."

I don't reply. He needs more time to absorb everything I have to say. I can't rush this.

"But you haven't been tapped?" he queries.

I wave my hand dismissively. "Yes, I have. Jeeves hid it with dark magic."

I ignore the implication I'm giving that it was my butler who tapped me. I don't care and it is not relevant. And I like that version more than I like the truth.

Drew's eyebrows almost disappear into his hairline. He collapses back into the chair.

"Well," he huffs.

"You have to help me!" I exclaim. The words burst out of me, bypassing my conscious thoughts. I wince, but it can't be helped now.

"Why do I have to help you?" he asks as he raises one sardonic eyebrow.

"Because you are a good person and it is the right thing to do. You are not a Revivalist, and you love adventure and I'm your favorite second cousin," I plead, and then hold my breath.

I give him my very best puppy-dog eyes and wait. He stares back at me. The clock on the mantelpiece ticks loudly.

"That is all true, Barny, but I'm sorry, I can't get involved. This is all too big."

I let out the breath I had been holding. I search his face for any signs that he might be tempted, that he might be wavering, and that all he needs is further nudging. But while I do see curiosity, intrigue, and a little temptation, mostly I just see resolution. He is not going to change his mind.

The bitter taste of disappointment floods my mouth, but I don't have time for that. I draw in another breath. I didn't want it to come to this, but it has.

"If you don't help me, I shall tell everyone that you are not the child of your mother's husband, but her own father's."

His face drains of all color. He looks truly stricken. Dazed. Hurt. Betrayed. As if the wind has been knocked out of him.

"How the hell do you . . ." he begins before shaking his head. "Nevermind. Why would you do such a thing?"

"Because the love of my life might be executed and I'm desperate."

I meet his gaze evenly. I bare my soul to him. I want him to see that I truly bear him no malice and that I am only driven to this out of sheer desperation. Desperation and love.

He sighs heavily and slumps back in his chair. "I've always been a sucker for romance."

My heart thuds. Hope starts to tingle through me and it makes me dizzy.

"You are going to help?"

"You haven't given me much choice."

I'm sure I will feel guilty later, when this is all over. At the moment, all I feel is elation that my plan is working.

Drew leans forward, picks up his cup of tea and takes a sip. I can almost see the cogs of his mind whirling. He has turned his attention to devising a plan. I want to rub my hands together in glee, but I resist. Rubbing his face in my victory would be cruel and only succeed in pissing him off. When, at the moment, it feels as if his compliance is led by a grudging respect for my devious nature. As well as his inherent love of adventure. Seems like he just needed a nudge, after all. Just a very forceful one.

"I'm assuming you picked on me as your victim because my parents are on the council?"

I nod. I'm not going to say anything to disrupt his flow of thought.

He sighs. "Sadly, my parents have nothing to do with the keeping of prisoners."

"But you must know someone who does?" I beg.

I'm not getting this far to give up at the first hurdle. It is not just his parents that Drew knows. By association, he is connected to most council members and workers, surely? Drew has to know someone who will know how to get in, and how to get Jeeves out.

I watch in anxious trepidation as he groans and closes his eyes. His head falls back against the chair.

"Yeah, I do," he admits reluctantly.

"Who?"

"The Mallory's," he says bitterly.

My heart starts to race. My mouth goes dry. This is brilliant. I have seen the way Lucien Mallory looks at his betrothed.

Drew pulls his phone out of his pocket. "Guess I'm arranging a meeting, then. With Lucien fucking Mallory."

Chapter Twenty-Six

The lights in my cell are blinding. Five sets of them. Four angled into each corner, and the fifth blasting from directly above. There are no shadows. Only plain white walls. White floor and ceiling. Does this mean they know I am a jin? Or is it simply psychological torture? I guess only time will tell.

It's also only time that will allow me to escape. I have a long life. I can spare some years, or decades. But Barny cannot. Will he wait for me? Will he be an old man by the time I'm free? I won't care, but I think it would worry him.

And what if the council knows I am a jin, and they decide to banish me? To imprison me truly?

A shudder wracks my body. Fear claws at me with its icy fingers. It cannot come to that. Being confined and inert for centuries is bearable. Emerging back into a world where even the memory of Barny has long faded, is not.

I have to do something. I have to get free.

But the wards here are thickly woven. Far surpassing my abilities. I can feel the sigils they have carved into my aura. Even if shadows were present, the magic will never let me pass the boundary. Regardless of what I do to the people keeping me here.

All I can do is wait. Wait and hope that something changes and an opportunity presents itself. And pray it happens before Barny forgets me.

Despair coils low within me. Nothing listens to my prayers. I know this. The universe is vast and endless, and in the great void there are no benevolent deities. At least, none that show themselves to me and my kind. Perhaps it is different for others.

The sudden presence of people on the other side of the door, pulls my attention away from my meandering thoughts. I think I will stay sat here, cross-legged on the floor, in the middle of the room, as if I don't have a care in the world. Or as if I'm too scared to move. They can read it as they wish.

They can stand and loom over me. In truth, I'm not scared of them. The worst they can do to me is keep me from Barny, and they are already doing that. But perhaps faking a little fear may help.

The woman who arrested me, Daphne, strolls into the room, accompanied by her usual henchmen. The heavy door locks shut behind them.

I look up at her and put on my best innocent expression. I have decided that pretending just to be a clueless human butler, is a card worth playing. At least until I have a better plan.

The harsh light overhead continues to cast a sterile glow on the featureless white walls that surround me. I put on a show of shifting uncomfortably in my spot on the floor, in this stark, empty room. Daphne stands before me, her piercing gaze fixed on my every move. Her voice cuts through the silence, each word dripping with suspicion.

"Richard Jeeves," she says, her tone cool and calculated, "Just answer the question, and maybe we can let you go."

She had asked me if I practiced dark magic before locking me in here, presumably to stew and loosen my tongue.

I meet her gaze, the intensity of her eyes making it clear that for her, this is no ordinary interrogation. She certainly suspects a lot of things. But not my name. That has to be a good sign. She is attempting to use my made-up, human full name as a power move. Which means she can't know the truth.

"I've told you, Daphne, I know nothing about dark magic. I'm not involved in anything like that," I protest, my voice echoing in the empty room. I had protested my innocence as she had slammed the door shut, and now I'm sticking to that story.

She raises an eyebrow, a silent challenge to the veracity of my words. "Richard, the evidence suggests otherwise. We've found artifacts in your possession, objects linked to forbidden rituals and dark incantations."

Now that's interesting. For two reasons. I hadn't realized that they had searched my room. And I don't need, use, or keep artifacts. Daphne could be bluffing, but I suspect that something else is going on. It looks like someone has tried very hard to set me up.

Challenge accepted. I can work with this and build a convincing story around it. Lies and manipulation are my oxygen. I will play this as a helpless human, out of his depth. A person who does keep strange belongings. Someone with dubious abilities that would arouse genuine suspicion, but isn't actually dangerous. Just a misunderstood outcast.

I'm not going to claim that my accuser is trying to frame me. I'm going to make it seem as if they made a well meaning mistake. It is the easiest path to take. Whoever my accuser is, they are likely to be trusted and respected by the council. Trying to convince them that this person has nefarious motivations would be an uphill battle. One that is not worth fighting.

I swallow hard, for show. "Those artifacts are family heirlooms! I had no idea they had any connection to dark magic. I swear!"

Daphne leans in, her gaze unwavering. "We've received reports, Richard. Witnesses have seen you practicing strange rituals, muttering incantations under your breath. You can't deny that there's something unusual about you."

Is she freely giving me information on purpose, or is she just incompetent at her job? Regardless, this new information changes nothing. I have more than one accusation against me, but that is fine. There is no need to change the story that I am building. Everything still fits.

I take a deep breath, and change my expression to one of frustration and fear.

"Unusual doesn't mean dark magic. I'm just different, that's all. I have abilities, yes, but they're not from any dark source."

It feels strange to not talk in the cadence and tone of my Jeeves persona, to play someone less confident, far warmer, and more easily flustered. I like being Jeeves. His character is like a worn and comfortable glove. It fits me well, like a second skin, and is far closer to my true nature than any other human character I have ever put on.

But Richard Jeeves is far more likable. And likable is much more likely to get me out of here. Humans are such simple creatures at heart. Easily swayed by charm and a pretty face.

She narrows her eyes, and for a moment I worry about her mind-reading abilities, but then I see that she is simply scrutinizing the words I spoke to her.

"Abilities? What kind of abilities, Richard? Be specific."

I hesitate, putting on a show of thinking that revealing too much could worsen my situation. Making everything seem too simple would not be convincing. There needs to be layers of complexity. Richard Jeeves needs to be trying to hide some things to save his own skin. It makes him more relatable.

"I can . . . sense things. Feel strange energies around me. Especially in shadows. It's not something I asked for. It's just there."

Daphne folds her arms, unimpressed. "That's not a satisfactory explanation, Richard. We need to know the source of your powers. We need to ensure you're not a threat to society."

I shake my head, and act as if frustration is mounting. "I'm not a threat! I'm just trying to live my life, just like everyone else. You can't keep me locked up like this based on suspicions and rumors."

Daphne remains unmoved, her gaze unwavering. "Prove it, then. Prove that your powers are harmless, that you're not dabbling in dark magic. Otherwise, we have no choice but to take more drastic measures."

As the weight of her words hangs in the air, I realize that my ploy for freedom is far from over. She is more demanding than I first gave her credit for. And so far, she seems rather immune to Richard Jeeves's charm. It's not a disaster. I can work with this, and I have a few more cards to play.

But first, I'm going to have to come up with a demonstration of magic that is dark enough to arouse suspicions, but not so dark as to alarm Daphne.

It is a good thing I have always enjoyed a challenge.

Chapter
Twenty-Seven

This gatehouse appears to be one large room. It's a little dusty and a little damp, and feels empty and unused. But the red carpet I'm pacing is good quality, so perhaps this place was loved once.

Drew is standing near a corner, away from the window, looking at me as if he is concerned for my sanity, but I don't care.

"How much longer is he going to be?" I snap.

Drew shrugs. "He said it would take him a while to sneak out unnoticed."

I glance at my watch. Three a.m. A sudden thought strikes me.

"Oh gods, he doesn't think you asked to meet for a tryst, does he?"

Drew shakes his head at me. "No idea what he is thinking. I couldn't exactly explain by text message and leave evidence."

My pacing stops and I stare at Drew in horror. How can anyone be so stupid? Sending covert messages to your betrothed, asking to meet up in secret in the middle of the night? Of course Lucien is going to think one thing. It is the same one thing that anyone would think.

"If he turns up in lingerie, I'm never speaking to you again!" I huff.

Drew lets out a snort laugh. "Lucien Mallory in lingerie? Have you met the man? It is about as likely as flying pigs. He'll turn up in a neatly pressed suit. I'll bet good money on it."

I scowl at him but say nothing. He is probably right. I can't imagine prim and proper Lucien even having a hair out of place. In fact, I can't picture him turning up for a midnight tryst at all. I swallow. Oh gods, what if he doesn't come?

Just as I am despairing, the front door opens with a creak, and I whirl to face it. Lucien steps in. His eyes flash with surprise when he sees me, but he says nothing. I bite back my bitter laugh, because he is indeed wearing a suit. A very nice dark blue one. At three a.m. For climbing out of his bedroom window and meeting his fiancé in the gatehouse.

He carefully shuts the door behind him and then looks expectantly at Drew. Waiting to be told what is required of him, like a perfect little vessel. I'm not sure if he came here out of willingness to please his future husband, or if he is simply that obedient.

Drew sighs as if the weight of the world is on his shoulders. "We need your help to break someone out of council custody."

Lucien's eyes widen and he moves his fidgeting hands to behind his back. "I'm afraid that is not possible, Count Felford."

"Bullshit. I know you know how to do it!" snaps Drew.

Lucien flinches and pales. It makes the deep green of his eyes stand out even more. "Your faith in me is flattering, my lord, but sadly I cannot help."

Drew's face twists into something deeply unpleasant. "In two months, you will belong to me. I'd suggest it is in your best interest to keep me happy."

Lucien's gaze hurriedly drops to the floor, and he starts to tremble ever so slightly. I lift my hand to whack Drew for being such a disgusting asshole, but then I freeze mid-motion. I need to free Jeeves. I will do whatever it takes. I've already resorted to blackmail. Standing by while Drew is a cruel, domineering asshole is a price I'm willing to pay. If that makes me a bad person, well, I guess I'm a bad person now.

My stomach still twists in revolt as I watch Lucien ponder his options. After a few heartbeats, his shoulders slump in defeat. Glee ignites alongside my guilt and I think I might throw up.

Lucien licks his lips. "Getting in is relatively straightforward. However, getting a prisoner out once they have been marked, is impossible."

"How do we remove the marks?" I ask.

Green eyes lift from the floor to look at me. "I'm really not sure if it can be done, Lord Rosewarne."

I think he sees something in my eyes, for he quickly takes another breath. "Tell me everything, so I know what we are working with."

Relief, hope, and countless nameless emotions all swirl through me. This might actually work. Lucien is clever and he has connections. He is familiar with the inner workings of the council.

I'm coming Jeeves. I'm coming, I breathe silently.

I can't believe I'm actually standing in the council chambers. It feels like a huge achievement, despite Lucien's insistence that this is the easy part.

I'm all but thrumming with anxiety and anticipation, and caffeine. Jeeves was taken two days ago and I have not slept a wink since. I should have rested during the day, as Lucien suggested. But sleep was impossible to find. Waiting for nightfall was the hardest thing I've ever done.

Rationally, breaking someone out of a busy and heavily guarded building, is going to be easier in the small hours of the night. But just sitting on my ass for long, long hours while Jeeves was likely being tortured, was awful. And now, I'm so very glad to finally be here and actually doing something. Even if my life is in peril.

Lucien pulls me into an empty office. The blinds are open, and the soft glow of streetlights dimly illuminates the room. He fidgets with the straps of his backpack.

"The guarded section is just up ahead," he whispers.

I nod my understanding.

He fidgets some more, and unease rolls off of him. Guilt flares briefly within me but is quickly extinguished by thoughts of Jeeves. I'm blackmailing Drew. Drew is bullying Lucien. But it is going to get Jeeves free, so I don't care.

"I'll distract the guards. Then the rest is up to you," he says.

I nod again. I know the plan. Lucien distracts the guards. I sneak in and get Jeeves and then run. Drew is waiting in a car down the road, but he won't be acting as a getaway driver, he will be creating a portal for our escape.

Lucien licks his lips. He is clearly hesitating. If he backs out now, I'm so screwed.

"You mustn't tell Count Felford about anything you see."

I nod my head in frustration. This delay is unnecessary. Lucien stares at me.

"Fine!" I hiss. Why the hell I'd talk to Drew about anything is beyond me. But whatever.

"Swear a vow," demands Lucien, his eyes bright in the dark.

"I, Barnaby Withywood-Lamont, do solemnly swear to never speak to anyone about what I see tonight." Whatever makes Lucien get a move on.

He bites his bottom lip, then nods. "Wait ten minutes and then approach the guard station carefully. If it is clear, go for it."

Then he is gone. Slipping out the door with enviable grace. I take a deep breath and stare at my watch. The second hand slows down to a barely perceptible movement. I huff impatiently. Ten minutes pass slower than ten millennia. But finally it is time to go.

I creep down the corridor. As I reach the guard station, I hear voices and my heart sinks. The path is not clear yet. Then I hear Lucien speak.

"Oh, thank you so much for the directions! I can't believe I got so lost! I'm so silly!" he gushes. His voice sounds somehow different, but it is clearly still him.

The guards laugh, and my brow furrows in puzzlement. Nothing he said was funny. I risk a peek around the corner and nearly gasp in astonishment.

I see a desk and two guards standing by it. Behind them is a set of plain double doors. If Lucien is right, they lead to the cells. But right now, it is Lucien that has my full attention.

He is wearing a very short purple skirt. And thigh-high black socks. A tight black crop top leaves his perfect midriff bare. A pair of purple, fluffy cat ears sit upon his head. He looks incredible. His figure is slender and almost feminine. That waist is the stuff wet dreams are made of. He looks like the world's sexiest femboy. Is he secretly a camboy? No wonder he doesn't want his future husband to know.

I stare transfixed as he twirls a lock of hair between his fingers. "Would one of you be kind enough to walk me to my car? I get scared when I'm all alone."

Both guards immediately volunteer. It makes me grin. I can't say I blame them. Lucien looks amazing. And femme enough to confuse even the straightest man.

I watch as Lucien leads them away. Is he going to be okay? He looks like a sex god, but he is an untapped vessel, and therefore a virgin. He can't have that much experience with men and how angry they can be when they feel they have been promised something.

My gaze flicks down the corridor after him, and then to the double doors. Fuck it. Lucien is going to have to look after himself. I'm here to free Jeeves.

I sprint down the hallway and through the double doors with a speed I did not know I possessed. I find cell six with no problem at all. The code Lucien told me to memorize works perfectly, and the door unlocks with a quiet beep. I push it open.

The sight of Jeeves fills my heart with sheer and utter joy. He looks unharmed. The plain, brightly lit room he is in looks awful. But there is no time for rage. There is no time for anything.

I yank the small silver bottle out of my pocket and unstopper it. Jeeves's dark eyes widen and he takes a step back.

"Please! I know it's awful, but it is the only way to get you out of here!"

My heart is pounding. My ears are straining to hear every slightest noise. I'm convinced any second now the alarm is going to be raised.

Jeeves's dark eyes flick between the ornate bottle and me.

"Please, Jeeves. Please trust me!"

He looks at me. Truly looks at me. His expression softens, and he nods.

I let out the breath I was holding.

Jeeves becomes shadow and smoke. He flies across the cell and pours into the bottle I am holding. I shove the stopper in, clench my fist tightly around the bottle, and turn on my heels.

Now it is time to run.

Chapter Twenty-Eight

My hands are trembling as I pull the small cork from the neck of the bottle. Immediately, dark smoke and shadow pour out. I blink, and then Jeeves is standing before me, his dark eyes intense. He looks far too wonderful for this plain and grimy room.

The curtains are drawn against the midday light. It is dim in here. Which helps hide the beige carpets and walls that I suspect were once white.

An eerie silence wraps over everything. It devours the outside world. Drowning out the hum of the city street. There is nothing but Jeeves and I staring at each other. I'm not even sure if I am breathing.

"How long?" he asks, each word heavy and laden. He is pissed off, and I don't blame him.

"Just over eight hours," I answer. I hated keeping him imprisoned for even that long. But I couldn't release him until I was absolutely sure it was safe to do so.

His stony expression does not shift.

"Where are we?"

I hate to see him so disoriented. So vulnerable. But the fact he is asking me rather than pretending that he already knows, gives me hope.

"In a dodgy hotel in Bristol, that let me pay in cash and didn't ask for I.D."

His gaze drops and locks onto the silver bottle in my hand. "Where did you get that from?"

I swallow. "Lucien Mallory. I needed his help to get you out of there."

Dark eyes flare. "He knows I am jin?"

"I'm sorry. I have . . . information on him that he does not want known."

Please let it be enough for Jeeves to forgive me for sharing his secret. I can't bear the thought of him feeling as if I have betrayed him by giving a stranger power over him.

Jeeves stares at me for three agonizing heartbeats. Then suddenly, he strides forward and wraps his arms around me. His embrace is strong. I'm pressed tightly against his firm chest and I have no wish to be anywhere else.

"Thank you, my love," he whispers.

My muscles give up, and turn to quivering jelly. Tears start to pour from me. I don't know why I'm crying and falling apart now that it is all over. Now that Jeeves is safe. Now that he has forgiven me.

He effortlessly moves us to the bed. We lie down and I cling to him as if I were the one who was locked up and tortured. He doesn't seem to mind. I suspect he much prefers the role of caregiver than cared for. And that is just fine by me.

Especially as, right now, I'm more concerned with confirming that this is not a dream. Did my plan really work?

I can feel him with my hands, fill my lungs with his sandalwood scent, see him with my eyes, and sense him with my magic, but it is still not enough to reassure myself that he is really here.

His body heat is seeping into me, and even this is not enough. I don't think I'm ever going to be able to let go of his embrace.

"Did they hurt you?" I sniffle, as the tears continue to fall.

I can't see any injuries, but I'm not so naïve as to think that means anything. The worst wounds leave no physical marks at all.

"No, my love," he whispers softly.

I sniffle again. "Would you tell me if they had?"

A smile lifts the corners of his mouth, and his dark eyes flood with warmth. "No, I would not," he admits.

I scowl at him, but I understand. He has his pride. He wishes to protect me. He is Jeeves, after all. It is just the way he is. I can let that question go.

"Will they be able to find you?" I ask.

Even speaking the question aloud makes my heart thump with terror. But I can't pretend it is not a possibility. Denial never solves a thing. Information and plans do.

"Not now that I know they are looking for me," he says.

I stare at him suspiciously. Is he speaking the truth, or is this merely more of what I need to hear?

"But you should return home soon, so they cannot pin any accusations against you."

A gasp of horror escapes me. My fingers twist in his shirt, securing my hold on him. Ice squeezes my lungs and I cannot breathe.

"I'm not leaving you!" I wail.

He runs a hand along my jaw, and I lean into his touch, chasing it. "We can discuss this tomorrow," he says.

My mouth opens and shuts several times. Then I nod. Tomorrow is soon enough. I will take it. It gives me the rest of the day with Jeeves. Tomorrow can wait. I refuse to think about anything else until then.

Jeeves is here, his arms are around me. It is all that matters. It is enough. It always will be.

"Do . . . do you need anything?" I ask hesitantly. "Did imprisonment deplete you?"

I'm not brave enough to clarify if I am referring to the council locking him up, or the imprisonment I subjected him to. I'm certainly not going to let on that I don't even know exactly what he might be depleted of. I know very little of my lover's nature. Does that make me a bad person, or a good one who respects his privacy?

"I'm fine, Barny. Truly. Just a little hungry."

"Oh, I don't think they do room service, but I could order pizza from a takeaway place?" I babble. "Do you even like pizza? We could get something else. Whatever you like."

What does Jeeves like to eat? What is his favorite food? Does he consider pizza for lunch uncouth? How can I be so madly in love with someone I know barely nothing about?

He cups my chin and smiles warmly, and every single doubt flies away. I may not know the fine details, but I know him. His essence. His aura. His soul.

"Pizza sounds wonderful," he says.

"Great!" I say as I pull my phone out of my pocket.

I'm not leaving this bed, or Jeeves's arms for anything. Even once the food arrives, we can eat pizza out of the box while sitting on the bed. Never mind not letting him out of my sight, I want some part of me touching some part of him for the rest of eternity. Forever does not sound long enough.

Worries about the future start to whisper at me. I try to shut them out, but there are too many of them.

I order the pizza and put my phone away. The simple action does not clear my mind.

It's going to be fine, I tell myself. Jeeves just has to disguise himself, and then we can be together. Or at the very worst, he won't be able to stay at Rocester Hall, but will be able to walk through the shadows to visit me. Hopefully every night.

It doesn't sound like enough. Nowhere near enough. I don't want Jeeves only at night. I want to spend every waking moment with him.

I take a deep breath and resolutely push all those thoughts away, as was my original plan. I'm not wasting precious time. Problems are for tomorrow. Today is for Jeeves.

Jeeves is here. Free and unharmed. I need to concentrate on that. And the fact that we are alone, and there is this surprisingly comfortable bed. It would be a shame not to make use of it. A great shame indeed.

Arousal starts to thrum within me. Low and heavy. Waking up, stirring, and igniting. Filling me with warmth.

I wonder how long the pizza is going to take?

I stare into Jeeves's dark eyes. The thought of being interrupted sounds like a nightmare. Besides, Jeeves said he was hungry. I can wait. We have the rest of the night, and I know exactly what I want to do to him.

His eyes flash and a very naughty smirk twists across his face. I grin back. I wonder just how many of my thoughts he has discerned? I hope not all of them. Not because I am ashamed, I suddenly realize, but because I would like to surprise him.

But in the meantime, lying here, holding him and being held by him, is a bliss I can tolerate. I can drink in the joy of this moment and keep it forever.

It is almost perfect.

Chapter Twenty-Nine

Folding empty pizza boxes and shoving them into the small bin is strangely satisfying. Eating pizza in bed with Barny was a joy like no other.

It felt almost like a dream. I think I'm still in shock that he came to rescue me. I'm not surprised about his ability, nor his tenacity. It is just that I've never had anyone care about me before. I've been utterly alone for long centuries. Being loved is a startling yet wondrous thing to adjust to.

My ears prick at the sound of the shower turning off. I turn to face the door just as Barny opens it. He is wearing nothing but a towel slung low across his hips. The rest of his body is naked for me to feast my eyes upon. And oh my, is it a sight to behold. He truly is beautiful. Inside and out.

Arousal consumes me, sudden and insistent. Nearly overwhelming. It turns the air between us heavy and charged. I'm not sure if I am breathing. I knew this was the plan. Food, then sex. And I have been looking forward to it. But now the moment is here, I'm blown away.

I'm about to make love to Barny. He is not ripe, there is no need to join our bodies. We simply hunger for one another.

"Can . . . can you take your clothes off, please?" he begs.

The desperate desire in his voice and in his eyes feeds my arousal. Barny yearns to see my body. I consider making a tease of undressing, but I don't have the patience for that. So I strip my clothes off efficiently and all but fling them across the room.

I stand naked before him and watch in satisfaction as his face fills with hunger and delight. He likes to look at me, and nothing has ever made me prouder. But this distance between us is unbearable.

I stride over to him, angle his head up, and kiss him. He moans softly and presses his body close to mine. I can feel his cock hardening as I claim his mouth. I love that he wants me so much that a simple kiss can fire his blood.

I wrap my arms around him and pull him with me as I step backward, toward the bed. As soon as my calves touch the bed, Barny pushes firmly down on my shoulders. I obey his wish and sit on the edge of the mattress. His little flare of dominance has ignited a deep and feral heat within me. The most primal part of me accepts the challenge, and hungers to put Barny in his place.

Barny drops to his knees, between my legs. I like this confident and eager side of him. It is most pleasing. His eyes darken as he stares appreciatively at my hard cock.

"It is a monster," he whispers, as if confirming a truth to himself.

I chuckle.

He looks up at me and licks his lips. "Can I? Is this okay?" His eyes are bright and a little unsure. It squeezes at my heart. He has to know there is not a reality in existence where I do not want his lips upon me.

"Very," I say as I run a hand through his silky hair.

He shudders and leans forward. My breath hitches and catches in my throat. Barny licks his lips again, takes a deep breath, and then his hot, wet tongue is lapping at my cock. Little tiny licks near the head, as if he is testing the taste and the texture. He moans and starts licking more confidently. Firmer, longer strokes of his divinely soft tongue.

Sensation overwhelms me. Pleasure burns. I groan. Barny answers with a needy whimper. He explores more of my cock, seemingly determined to run his tongue over every single part of it.

He is doing incredibly well for his first time.

He works his way back up to the head. His lips stretch, and he takes the very tip of my cock into his warm, wet mouth. My fingers tighten in his hair and he groans. He lowers his head and takes more of me. His mouth is so hot. His tongue twitches on the underside of my cock. I stare down at him and watch his swollen lips glide further and further down my cock. His eyes are closed and he looks blissed out.

I reach the back of his throat and he gags a little, but tries again. I stop him with a gentle pull of his hair. There is no way he will be able to take me all on his first time. I'm honored that he wishes to try.

"Put your hand around what you can't fit in," I say, and my voice is low. Pretty much a growl.

Barny quickly complies, and I gasp. He feels incredible. I can barely believe this is happening. Barny is on his knees before me, working hard to pleasure me.

He experiments for a moment and finds a rhythm that makes my thighs tremble. His head bobs up and down my cock, his hand caresses my base. I let my head fall back and I allow myself to feel.

He moans as if my cock is the most delicious thing he has ever tasted, and the sound of his enjoyment is music to my ears. The most divine sound I have ever heard.

"Barny," I rumble. "I'm going to . . ." I can't draw in enough breath to finish that sentence, but I think he understands.

To my astonishment, he doesn't pull away. Instead, he starts sucking my cock with increased fervor. The pressure, the tightness, is exquisite. My euphoria pours out of me. An orgasm rushes through me. My cock pulses. The sound of Barny swallowing, all but destroys me. All my senses dim. All I can feel is the pleasure Barny has given me.

After a long moment, awareness settles back over me. My head is tipped back and I'm panting heavily. Barny is still on his knees but slumped to the side, resting his head on my thigh.

His magic itches along my skin and seeps into my soul. I lift my head and look down at him. He opens his eyes and looks up at me. His cheeks are flushed.

"I came too," he says in a tone of shocked surprise.

I grin and pull him up onto the bed. "That is very flattering, my love."

He squirms in delight as I arrange us properly on the bed, lying side by side with our heads on the pillows.

"I wanted you to take me," Barny says wistfully.

I pull him close and kiss the top of his head. "Give me but a moment, my love."

"Really?"

I chuckle at the delighted surprise in his voice.

"Sorry!" Barny exclaims. "I didn't mean to imply that I think you are old or anything."

I roll to my side so I can see him better. "I know, my love. I know you are very new to all of this."

He blushes again, and I lean forward and kiss him. He squeaks in surprise but soon melts into it, and kisses me back with a hunger that is exhilarating.

He whimpers when I pull away.

"Roll onto your stomach, for me," I breathe.

His eyes flash and he immediately does as I bid. Grinning, I slide down the bed until my head is level with his wonderful ass.

He takes in a shuddering breath. "What . . . what are you doing?" His nervous excitement fans the flames of my arousal.

"I'm going to fuck you with my tongue."

He gasps and his hips lift a little, offering himself to me. The sight sets my very soul on fire.

I pull his perfect ass cheeks apart and dive right in. He squeals and squirms, but it is no effort at all to hold him in place. My tongue slurps eagerly over and around his hole. The taste of him is incredible. I will never, ever be able to get enough.

I lap, I flick, I swirl. Barny whines, whimpers, and wails. I stiffen my tongue and slide into him. Deeper than a human could go. He screams in ecstasy. His hips buck frantically. I deliver my promise and flick my dripping wet tongue in and out of him with as much speed as I can muster.

He screams again. Twisting desperately. He yowls. Then his back arches as every muscle in his body clenches. He comes hard. Harder than I've ever seen anyone come. But

I show no mercy. I keep going. He is a young human man, and a vessel. My tongue can reach his prostate and right now, his is swollen with arousal and pleasure. I toy with it and Barny sobs and sobs and then spills again. Silently this time.

I release him and he sags boneless against the sheets, panting heavily. Sweat is beading his back, strengthening his delicious scent.

I lean over him, covering his body with my own. I lower my head and trace the shell of his ear with my tongue. He moans and shivers weakly.

"Are you ready for me to fuck you now, my love?" I whisper.

His hands clench the sheets and he lets out an incoherent string of gibberish. I think there are some swear words.

A grin stretches across my face. It was very clearly a yes.

Tonight is going to be wonderful.

Chapter Thirty

The various sounds of this coffee shop are blurring together to make a soothing background hum. We are sitting by the window, and late summer sunlight is streaming in and illuminating Barny's golden hair. He looks wonderful. He always does.

There are slight, dark circles under his eyes and they make me perversely proud. I tired him out and worked him hard last night, and it was glorious. Memories of those amazing hours crowd at the corner of my mind, but I keep them at bay. Now is not the time. Now is the time for drinking in new memories to cherish forever. Not basking in ones that I have already collected.

Barny brings his ridiculously huge coffee cup to his lips, and he smiles at me, his blue eyes flashing. I smile back, helplessly enthralled. He is dressed informally today, we both are. And the casual look of tee shirt and jeans looks damn fine on him.

He looks his age. He doesn't look like an earl, with all the responsibility that station comes with. He doesn't look like a vessel, with the duty, expectations, and oppression that role carries with it.

Right here, right now, he appears as a young human. Free to make his own choices in life. It suits him immensely. He looks happy. At ease. Someone who is master of their own destiny.

I cast a quick glance around all the mundanes in the coffee shop. If only they appreciated all that they have. It is a shame that they don't even know how lucky they are. A normal life is the most precious gift of all.

Suddenly, my guts twist. Ice pulls at them and nearly takes my breath away. The pain of it scatters all other thoughts from my mind. I quickly hide my grimace by bringing my coffee cup to my face, but I cannot deny the truth any longer. My masters are trying to summon me. This precious, stolen time with Barny is over.

"Let's go for a walk," I say.

I can steal one more hour, surely. My masters are no doubt furious, but Barny deserves an explanation. And a farewell.

My heart forgets how to beat for a moment, and then restarts with a shudder. I don't want to leave him. The pain of it is going to destroy me. But there is no choice. I would do anything, absolutely anything to keep Barny safe. My own suffering is but a small price to pay.

Barny smiles and gets to his feet. "Sounds lovely."

We leave the coffee shop and amble through the bustling city streets in comfortable silence. It doesn't take long to reach the park. I watch Barny as he takes it all in. The brightly colored flower beds, the picnicking couples, the playing children, and the sunbathing office workers on their lunch break.

Barny grins at me, his face full of delight. He takes my hand, and my soul twists in anguish. He is too bright, too precious for this world. He is capable of seeing joy in the smallest of things. And I am about to hurt him.

Devastate him. All for his own good, but as I know full well, intention will not lessen his pain.

We walk a little further and find a spot where the park slopes down sharply, revealing a stunning view of the city spread out before us. Barny makes a soft noise of appreciation at the sight as we stop to admire it.

For a moment, it feels as if I cannot do it. I don't have the strength. I'm too weak. Then I look at him grinning at the view, for all the world like a child in a sweet shop, and I find my resolve. I can be ruthless. It is my nature. I can do what needs to be done. I always have. I will not fail now, when it is more important than ever.

Barny must be kept safe. It is imperative. It is the only thing that has ever mattered.

I look blindly out at the vista before me. It is as good a spot as any, and I cannot delay the inevitable for any longer.

"Thank you for freeing me," I say. Easing in with an explanation seems like a good way to begin. Or perhaps I need to build up my courage. Maybe it's both.

His brow scrunches in puzzlement. "Of course," he replies, almost distractedly. His eyes are still fixed on the view.

I shake my head. "Not just from the council."

He looks up at me, giving me his full attention and patiently waiting for me to continue.

I clear my throat. "The act of sealing me in a bottle, and then releasing me, has greatly diminished the hold others have over me."

Alarm flares across Barny's face, and I long to kiss it away.

"What others?" he demands.

My heart stutters. Dismay and regret twist through me. There are so many things I wish I could say. So many foolish choices I wish I could undo.

"I wish I could tell you." Are the only words that pass my lips.

He stares at me for a heartbeat. Then he swallows and nods a clearly reluctant agreement. He trusts me. He accepts my judgment. His grip on my hand tightens, and I relish the feel of it. Barny does not want to let me go.

"They won't let me go. They will hunt me. As will the council," I say, even though they are the last words on Earth that I wish to be speaking.

Barny snatches his gaze away, but not before I catch a glimpse of his pained expression. I have hurt him. I have caused him suffering, and the pain of that is far worse than any torture I have ever endured.

"What are you saying?" he asks weakly.

I take a deep breath. "That I need to flee. I will take you home first, but then I must leave, and I do not know when I will be able to return."

Barny's hold on my hand tightens to a death grip, but I don't mind at all. He doesn't say anything, he doesn't look at me. I think he is fighting tears. He already knew that I would need to hide from the council. He understood that our moments together would be fleeting. But my revelation that even that is not possible, must be hard to hear.

"I'm going to hunt them in return," I try to reassure. "I will eliminate my enemies and secure my true freedom so that I may return to you and stay by your side forever."

His blue eyes finally turn to mine, and they are full of tears.

"Can they kill you?"

I open my mouth to lie to him, to give him false promises, anything to stop his tears. But he deserves better than that. Barny deserves as much truth as I can give him.

"They can banish me, which is more or less the same thing."

He lets out a heartfelt, anguished sob, and the sound shatters my heart into a thousand pieces.

"So you are leaving and I might never see you again?" he wails in distress.

It is too much. Far too much. I cannot bear to see him like this. It is the worst torment I have ever known.

I pull him into my arms, press him against my chest, and kiss him. It is a feeble, temporary fix, but it is the only thing I can give my sweet, precious boy. It is but one, small way that I can offer some comfort and try to chase his pain away.

His arms entwine around my neck. He kisses me as if I am the only source of oxygen in the whole entire world. Someone lets out a wolf-whistle, but I don't care. Right now I'm kissing Barny, and it might be our last kiss.

Nothing else matters.

Chapter Thirty-One

I t is a little creepy in this alleyway, even though it is still daylight. But Jeeves told me to wait here, so I know it is safe. He is getting a car, so he shouldn't be too long. I need to use this time to gather my thoughts and my resolve. Practicing what to say would also be a good idea.

It's a shame that my heart is pounding like a crazed rabbit's, and my mouth is dry. It is making it hard to think at all. Let alone rehearse articulate words.

But I'm not going to let myself spiral into panic. I'm going to hold on to the look on Jeeves's face as he left me here. He didn't want to. He hated having to do it.

It has to mean that he doesn't truly wish to leave me forever. I am going to be able to change his mind. I have to. Nothing has ever been so important. I need to say the right things. I need to get this right. My life might as well be over if I don't.

Suddenly, the deep rumble of a motorbike engine reverberates around the walls of the alley. It makes me jump. I look up and feel my eyes nearly bug out of my head. It is Jeeves, riding a slick black motorbike. He is even wearing tight black leathers. I think I'm going to asphyxiate from lust. No one in the history of the universe has ever looked hotter.

I don't even care how or where he got the bike and the clothes. What's a little crime when the end result is so drool-worthy?

He pulls up beside me and grins. He tosses a black helmet at me, and I fumble to catch it. Because, yeah, Jeeves is a sex god and I am a bumbling idiot.

"Let's go," he says.

My imagination jumps to life. I see myself on the back of Jeeves's bike. Every part of me pressed up close to him. My arms wrapped tightly around his waist. The throb of the motorbike between my legs and the air rushing past.

I swallow. Then take a deep breath and steel myself.

"You are not taking me to Rocester Hall."

His smile falters at my words. He raises one eyebrow. "Pardon?"

My heart skips a beat. "I'm going with you," I say with a confidence I am not feeling. I think my voice only shook a little.

Jeeves sighs sadly. Pain clear in his dark eyes. "You can't leave your life."

"What life?" I snap. Then I pause and attempt to pull myself together. "I can leave my life, and I will. You are a million times more important than anything else I have."

He looks away from me. "It is too dangerous."

"Leaving me behind is even more dangerous," I plead. "Wyesdale might seek revenge or another attempt."

Jeeves's dark eyes snap back to me, now blazing with fury. A truly terrifying scowl is twisting his face. "He has learnt his lesson."

"You are assuming that he has the intelligence to learn and that he is not deranged. Or that no one else will have the same idea."

Jeeves says nothing. His expression is still fierce. I think he may be wavering.

"Then there is the council," I add as another shot.

Jeeves has escaped from their custody. It would be very strange if they did not at least question me about it. Surely he can see that?

He stares back at me, and I cannot read his expression. I have no idea what he is thinking.

Doubt starts to gnaw at me. Why is he being so resistant, so stubborn? Does he not want me? Is his whole "leaving to protect me," merely a hollow excuse?

A long, tense silence stretches. The walls of the alley seem to lean in and the very air becomes heavy. Our gazes are locked. My eyes are brimming with tears. His are revealing nothing.

Eventually, Jeeves sighs heavily. "It is far too dangerous for you to come with me. It will anger my former masters and alarm any who know what you are."

I stare blankly at him. I wasn't expecting him to say that. Wyesdale's voice echoes in my head. He had said something frightfully similar. He had implied that I am something.

"What am I?" I ask in a trembling voice. I'm not sure I even want to know.

Jeeves gives me a tormented look that makes my guts twist. He really does not want to say what he is about to say.

"You are a strong genetic throwback to fey ancestry."

Every remotely coherent thought I have ever formed falls right out of my head.

"I'm fey?" I croak in sheer and utter disbelief.

Jeeves nods. I understand. There really are no words for this.

"You knew this, and you didn't tell me?" My voice is pained. I cannot begin to comprehend the full implications of what he has told me. But tendrils of meaning are lancing through my heart.

Jeeves's beautiful dark eyes fill with sorrow and regret. Enough to drown an ocean.

"I was not permitted to," he whispers.

I close my eyes against the pain. Jeeves is a jin, he has masters. Masters who had even more of a hold over him than they do now. It was not his choice to betray me. He did not have free will.

"Fine," I breathe on an exhale.

Sheer astonishment sparkles in Jeeves's eyes and flows across his face. "I lied to you. You should hate me."

What a ridiculous idea. A smile takes over my lips. "I could never hate you."

Jeeves looks completely thunderstruck, and I hate that being loved is such a new and unknown thing to him. It makes me determined to make him accustomed to it. Jeeves is wonderful. He needs to know it.

"Take me with you. Let us be together," I plead.

Jeeves takes a breath, but then releases it without saying anything. He lowers his gaze to the floor and shakes his head.

My fists clench by my sides. "Damn you, Jeeves! Don't make me beg, because I will!"

His shoulders hunch, but he does not look at me.

I take a long, shaky breath. I have one last card to play. One last chance to get my way.

"If you leave me, who is going to empty me?"

Dark eyes are suddenly boring into me. Still unfathomable, but at least he is looking at me. I take a deep breath and continue.

"You said there were other ways, but there was never any time for you to teach me. And it seems to be a terrible secret that I shouldn't know. So that leaves me with the traditional way. And I don't want anyone else. I only want you."

My words echo around the alley. I can read Jeeves's expression now. He looks horrified. Furious. He either hadn't thought of this before or had been trying very hard not to. I think this might work.

Elation starts to flow in my veins. Along with a little bit of guilt. But I would do absolutely anything to get my way on this. So what's a little manipulation? It's not as if I'm lying. I mean every heartfelt word I just spoke.

Now I just need to drive the truth home.

"Could you really lie there, hiding in some grotty hotel room, knowing that another man has his hands on me?"

A strange noise comes out of Jeeves. Deep and rumbling. I think it is a growl. His knuckles whiten on the handlebars of the bike. His eyes glow and dark smoke seeps off of him. I probably should be terrified, but it is my lust that is awoken, not any self-preservation skills.

"Get on the bike," he orders. Each word snapping around the alley.

My feet step forward, obeying him before I have had a chance to think a single thought. I swallow. Defeat tastes bitter. I should never have tried to goad him. Parting on bad terms is beyond awful.

"You are taking me to Rocester Hall?" I ask tearfully.

I cannot bring myself to call it home. It won't be home if Jeeves is not there. It will merely be an empty house.

Jeeves's eyes flash again. "No," he says sternly. "You are mine."

My heart stops as every part of me focuses on ensuring that I have heard and understood him correctly. I stare into his eyes and see the truth. My heart starts up again. Beating far too fast, but I don't care.

I shove the helmet onto my head and fling myself onto the back of the bike. I press myself as close to Jeeves as I can get and I wrap my arms around him. I'm grinning so broadly my face is hurting.

The bike roars to life between my legs. We race out of the alleyway and onto the open road. The speed is exhilarating, as is the joy of a new life. I feel like I am flying. It worked. I did it.

What was going to be the worst day ever, has become the first day of the rest of our life.

Jeeves and I, together forever.

What to Read Next.

Find out how to get a bonus epilogue of Jeeves & Barny enjoying life on the run, on the next page.

You can find Uncle Will & Jem's story in The Prince's Vessel.
And Duke Sothbridge & Colby in Duke Sothbridge's Vessel.
Lord Garrington & his not-brother are in Lord Garrington's Vessel.

Coming soon

Count Felford's Vessel

"Do you, Lucien Alexander James Mallory, take Count Felford to be your lord and master? Do you solemnly vow to honor and obey his every word?"

The words ring out clearly in the small chapel. My knees hurt. The flagstone floor is unyielding and cold.

"I do," I say, and I do not know how I got the words out.

"Do you, Count Felford, solemnly swear to take this vessel as your own and provide for his needs?"

"I do." Count Felford's voice is loud and clear.

He places is hand on the top of my head and I look up at him as I am supposed to. As usual, his stunning good looks make my heart flutter, and the disdain in his eyes twists my guts.

He still doesn't like me. Seven long years of engagement, and I have tried everything. I have been the best possible vessel I could be. I even helped him with his latest hairbrained scheme, and it has all been for nothing.

I would want any husband my parents chose, to like me. People are far kinder to those they are fond of. But I especially wanted Count Felford to like me, and I don't know why.

But it clearly isn't meant to be. Added to whatever flaws he sees in me, he doesn't like that I was chosen for him when he was sixteen, and there is not a thing I can do about that.

He hates me. He doesn't want me. He resents me. And he doesn't even know any of my secrets. How much worse will things be if he finds out?

"Blessed Be," chants the priest.

"Blessed Be," answers the congregation.

I swallow. It is done. I am bound to Count Felford. I am his property to do with as he chooses. I belong to a man who sneers in disgust every time he sees me.

I can look away now, but I don't. I'm caught in his dark gaze, like a rabbit in headlights. Or a mouse before a snake.

In a few short hours, this man is going to take me upstairs. He is going to take my body. Take my magic.

I have never been more terrified.

Want more?

Thank you so much for reading my book, it means the world to me!
I'd love to stay in touch. I have a monthly newsletter that comes with a bonus epilogue of Jeeves & Barny enjoying life on the run.

https://www.srodman.net/newsletter-sign-up.html

(If you are an existing subscriber, please click the link to the welcome pack that is at the bottom of all my emails.)
If newsletters aren't your thing, you can follow me on Amazon.
https://author.to/SRodmanAmazonPage

Thank you!

Books By S. Rodman

For an up-to-date list, you can view my Amazon Author
page HERE
Or view at www.srodman.net

Darkstar Pack

Evil Omega

Evilest Omega

Evil Overlord Omega

Duty & Magic: MM Modern Day Regency

Lord Garrington's Vessel

Earl Hathbury's Vessel

The Bodyguard's Vessel

Duke Sothbridge's Vessel

The Prince's Vessel

Found & Freed: The Unfettered

Unfettered Omega

Unfettered Kelpie

Non Series

All Rail the King

Shipped: A Hollywood Gay Romance

Hunted By The Omega

DragonKin

DragonRider

DragonSeer

DragonKing

Hell Broken

Past Life Lover

How to Romance an Incubus

Lost & Loved

Dark Mage Chained

Prison Mated

Incubus Broken

Omega Alone